AN UNNATURAL BEANSTALK

A RETELLING OF JACK AND THE BEANSTALK

BRITTANY FICHTER

THE ENTWINED TALES VOL. 2

AN UNNATURAL BEANSTALK: A RETELLING OF JACK AND THE BEANSTALK, ENTWINED TALES VOL. 2

An Unnatural Beanstalk / Brittany Fichter. -- 1st ed.

Cover Art and Design by Myrrhlynn and Page Nine Media

Edited by Meredith Tennant

~

To Paige

I'm so proud of you, my beautiful baby cousin. Whenever you find a new dream, you put your whole self into chasing it, giving it your all and never going halfway. Don't forget to slow down sometimes and let your family love on you the way you deserve to be loved. I believe firmly that God has a destiny for you, and that no one can fill the role you were given from eternity past.

ENTWINED TALES

1. A Goose Girl: Retelling of The Goose Girl - KM Shea

2. An Unnatural Beanstalk: A Retelling of Jack and the Beanstalk - Brittany Fichter

3. A Bear's Bride: A Retelling of East of the Sun, West of the Moon - Shari L. Tapscott

4. A Beautiful Curse: A Retelling of the Frog Bride - Kenley Davidson

5. A Little Mermaid: A Retelling of The Little Mermaid - Aya Ling

6. An Inconvenient Princess: A Retelling of Rapunzel - Melanie Cellier

THE WORLD OF THE ENTWINED TALES

PROLOGUE

NICE TRY, SISTER

*E*va held her breath as she hurried to pull the strings off the parchment wrapping. Then she and her sisters gasped as she lifted the sky-blue gown into the air.

"Oh, Eva!" Rynn breathed, giving Eva's shoulders a squeeze. "It's perfect!"

"Put it on! Put it on!" Sophie shoved Eva toward the dressmaker's little stall in the back of the shop. Eva obeyed, for once not rebuking her younger sister's impatience. Eva was just as excited to see it as Sophie.

The layers of blue silk caressed her skin like water as Mrs. Thatcher slid the dress down over Eva's head and shoulders and let it fall to her ankles. Eva closed her eyes and basked in the hundreds of soft ruffles as the dressmaker buttoned up the back of the gown.

"What do you think of the crystals?"

"Pardon me?"

Mrs. Thatcher laughed. "Look at your skirt."

Eva opened her eyes again and looked down more carefully this time, running her hands over the skirt's smooth surface. Sure enough, she felt rough little bumps where the gown flounced out just above the knees. She hadn't noticed them before because of the shade of the stall. But as soon as she stepped back into the window's light, the dozens of little crystals threw rainbows all across the room.

"There." Mrs. Thatcher sat back and gave a satisfied nod. "Go show your sisters."

As Eva stepped out from behind the curtain, she kept her eyes on the dress, hoping they wouldn't see her blush.

"Eva, you look like a fairy," Ellie called from her chair in the corner.

Eva gave a rueful laugh. "Is that a compliment?"

Ellie shrugged and went back to reading her book. "No. Just a fact."

Eva shook her head with a smile and hurried over to the full-length mirror in the corner. But as soon as she did, she put her hand self-consciously to her neck. "Why is the neckline so low?"

"My dear, isn't that what you wanted?" Mrs. Thatcher mumbled as she sat on the floor beside Eva and touched up some of the hem at the bottom of the gown.

"I'm afraid not. I had hoped for the design with the lace that came to the bottom of the throat."

Mrs. Thatcher took the pins out of her mouth and looked up with a confused frown. "I'm so sorry. But after you finished the last fitting I received your note saying you wanted the neckline to be lower. It even had your personal stamp."

Eva and Rynn exchanged a glance. "Sophie!" they said.

"What?" Sophie's brown eyes were large and innocent. But after her older sisters continued to frown at her, she finally rolled her eyes and crossed her arms. "Oh, fine. Yes, I might have helped Mrs. Thatcher finish the dress a tad more appropriately for the occasion. But it was only for your good!"

"For my good?" Eva leaned forward and cringed when she realized how careful she would have to be when bending over in this particular dress. "I'm supposed to be playing the harp for the Winter Ball. Not attracting every desperate man in Astoria!"

"It really isn't that bad," Rynn said, adjusting a few of the skirt's ruffles. "It's not a crime to show your collarbone." But then she turned to Sophie. "Keep this up, however, and next time I might call you-know-who to fix *your* dress."

Sophie smirked. "He wouldn't dare."

Penny peeked out from behind the corner, her amethyst eyes wide. "Be careful, Sophie. He hasn't gifted anyone in several years. Tempt him too much, and I doubt he'd pass up a chance to gift *you*."

Eva took another step back and evaluated her reflection once more. As much as she hated to admit it, Sophie's adjustment to her gown really *was* elegant. Though the gown didn't lessen Eva's obvious height, it succeeded in making her look graceful. The silken sleeves that reached to her wrists and ended in uneven shreds of wispy gauze sprinkled with dots of silver made her look closer to Ellie's delicate form than ever before. The bodice was also sprinkled with flecks of crystal, and its waist closed in a V that tapered gently into the full skirt.

For the first time since she'd hit her last growth spurt, Eva felt pretty.

After thanking Mrs. Thatcher over and over again, Eva changed out of the beautiful dress and watched longingly as the dressmaker wrapped it up once more. Just as she was getting ready to finish paying for the gown, however, the little bell above the door rang.

"Please excuse me, ladies." Mrs. Thatcher bustled out from behind the counter. "I'll be back in just a moment."

The sisters watched as Mrs. Thatcher hurried over to the newest customer. The customer, who looked vaguely familiar to Eva, was wearing a strange assortment of clothes, from a dress that was obviously too wide and too short, to shoes that fell off her heels every time she took a step. The young woman slowly pulled something from a basket. They couldn't see what it was, but the girls could see Mrs. Thatcher sadly shaking her head and placing a hand on the girl's cheek.

"Isn't that Elizabeth White?" Liesa whispered, appearing from behind a pile of wool.

"And where have you been?" Eva asked, handing Rynn her necklace so she could help Eva put it back on.

Liesa made a face at her older sister. "You know everything's not about you. If you must know, I was looking for a fabric for my new dress."

"Oh, so you're going to be playing harp with me?" Eva snickered. "I'll be sure to tell Mother that you want to practice tomorrow."

Liesa looked as though she wanted to make a smart retort, but the door closed again and Mrs. Thatcher returned.

"I apologize, girls, but that was Elizabeth White."

"Really?" Eva squinted at the young woman's retreating form through the window. "I haven't seen her for years. I thought she'd moved out of town."

Mrs. Thatcher nodded. "She did, but her family moved back last year when she got engaged to a young blacksmith at the edge of the city." The dressmaker sighed. "It's just so sad."

"What is?" Penny asked.

"She came to tell me that there was a fire at her parents' house last night. They lost everything. She was hoping I could repair her wedding gown, but the poor thing was just too far gone."

"When is her wedding?" Eva asked. She had a sinking feeling in her stomach.

Mrs. Thatcher ran her fingers nervously back and forth over a bolt of fabric on the cutting table. "Three days. Even if I had the material for the gown, which I would have to special order from a traveling merchant, I would need at least a week to finish a new dress that was even half as fine as the one she lost."

Eva forced a smile and quickly paid for her dress. Even as she did, however, she felt a small part of her heart breaking in two. She had waited for this gown for so long. But only when she'd been given the honor of being invited to be the main harpist at the city's

Winter Ball had she felt right in asking her parents for such an expensive gift. Not that they couldn't afford it. But there was something special about earning one's frivolities, and after all the years of her parents putting up with her excessive and sometimes awful music practice, Eva had felt as though this invitation had finally confirmed what she had so long wanted to believe. Not only did she consider herself a musician but finally, it seemed the world did, too.

Only now, with each second that she clutched the package to her chest, she became more aware of what she had to do. She walked even faster down the road.

"Why are you in such a hurry?" Sophie called as Eva's sisters caught up. "I told you I want to go to the little summer fair over on the other side of the market square. You can see it from here."

"I can see it, too!" Liesa bounced up and down on her toes. Then she stopped, and a sly grin crossed her face. She tapped Sophie on the shoulder. "It seems as if we are not the only ones looking."

"What you talking about?" Eva asked absentmindedly as she scanned the square.

"How do you *not* see him?" Sophie giggled. "Elmer Castings is standing at the edge of the crowd, and he's looking right at you, Eva."

Liesa elbowed Sophie. "It's a good thing you lowered that neckline. I hear Elmer's going to be at the Winter Ball, too."

"Elmer," Sophie pitched her voice up high, "you're such a man! Let's get married and have lots of babies! Then I can teach them all how to play the harp and boss everyone else around!" Then she and Liesa began to make kissing sounds before collapsing into one another's arms in fits of laughter.

"Elmer Castings smells like goat cheese," Ellie said as she joined them, still without looking up from her book. "It's because he spends too much time in the barnyard when he's supposed to be in the counting house with his father."

Penny watched them for a moment before shaking her head and

turning to Rynn and Eva. "Ellie's right. Elmer does smell like cheese. Still," she tilted her head thoughtfully, "I could use a few new bottles of ink, and I've heard they'll be selling colored ink at the fair today. Could we go for just a few minutes?"

Eva shook her head, still searching the crowd. "I promised Mother we would be home as soon as we were done at the dress shop. She needs help preparing for her dinner party tonight."

"Ellie, honey, could you give us a minute?" Rynn asked, her eyes fixed on Eva's face. As soon as Ellie had rolled her eyes and joined the others, Rynn leaned in. "Eva, I know what you're doing. And I don't think it's a good idea."

"How can you know that?" Eva tried to make her voice nonchalant.

"Because I'm your older sister. And what you're doing is kind, but it's unwise."

Eva finally quit searching and turned to face her sister. "But it's her wedding!"

"Penny was right. He hasn't been here in a long time. That girl is going to cause a ruckus. She doesn't know the meaning of quiet. And if you do this, she'll make a scene, and there's a good chance he'd take notice."

"Please," Ellie, who apparently had been listening in, peered around Rynn, "don't do it, Eva. I have a bad feeling about this!"

"Didn't Elizabeth call you Lumber Man for the entire year you were ten?" Sophie piped.

"It doesn't matter." Eva looked down at the package in her hands. "No one should be without a dress for her wedding." She looked back up at Rynn. "I'll be quiet about it, I promise! He'll never even know." Then, before Rynn could make a response, Eva spotted the young woman. "There she is!"

She hurried across the busy square before she had the chance to lose her nerve, bumping into several people along the way. When she reached Elizabeth, Eva shoved the gown into her arms. It nearly killed her, but if she didn't let go now, she never would. "Here," she said awkwardly. "Just . . . just don't tell anyone it was from me. Please!"

Elizabeth stared at the package then tore open the corner. When she saw what was inside, her green eyes looked as if they might fall out of her head. Without a word to Eva, she turned and started running, shrieking at the top of her lungs.

"Mother! Mother, look what Eva gave me!"

Eva stood there staring after her. "Well, that was . . . different," she said as Rynn came to stand beside her.

"You'll keep it quiet, huh?" Rynn frowned, but before Eva could say anything, a deafening *bang* came from behind them. The other girls ran up to join them just as a dreaded familiar face appeared in the middle of the square, balanced precariously on the fountain.

"All six of you again?" The fairy scowled. "Do any of you ever do anything by yourselves? No, don't answer that." He glared at Sophie. "Especially you. We all know what *you* do when you have time to waste."

"Mortimer, why are you here?" Rynn crossed her arms. "None of us called you."

"You think I don't know that? Believe me, if I didn't have to be here I wouldn't." He rubbed his stubbly chin and looked around until he spotted Eva. "What's all this fuss about?"

"Uh . . ." Eva stuttered, but Rynn stepped in front of her.

"She was just saying hello to an old friend."

Mortimer looked at Eva then back at Elizabeth, who was still screeching for her mother at the top of her lungs. He scowled again. "Didn't that girl call you Lumber Man when you were little?"

Eva threw up her hands in exasperation. "So I had a growth spurt! Is that all *anyone* remembers from that year?"

He rolled his sleeve up and scratched his ear thoughtfully. Then he froze and looked directly at Eva. "Did I ever give you any gifts?"

"Don't answer him, Eva," Leisa whispered. "It's a trap."

"So..." Mortimer frowned, "what kind of stuff do you like?"

"That's very kind of you, but I really don't need anything." Eva glanced around at the growing crowd that was surrounding them. People were beginning to point and whisper amongst themselves.

"Truly," Rynn said. "You really don't need to do this." She fixed him with a glare. "I mean it. Just . . . just let her reward be the satisfaction of having done something kind." The other girls nodded behind them.

Mortimer shook his wings out and cracked his knuckles. "Nice try, sister. The fairy council has been chasing my tail about ignoring your pathetic family for too long. If I do this, consider yourselves attended to for another year or so." He hopped off the fountain and walked up to Eva, his robes swishing in sharp, agitated movements. "Aren't you the harp player?"

Eva's mouth went dry.

But he just nodded to himself. "And doesn't your family have a thing for farming?"

"Woodcutting," Eva managed to whisper.

But Mortimer was already walking in a circle nodding to himself again. "So . . . farming and a harp. Farming and a harp." He snapped his fingers. "I've got it."

Sophie stepped forward. "Mortimer, mark my words. If you do this to Eva, I will haunt you every day until you remove the curse!"

Mortimer snorted. "It's not a curse, it's a gift. Besides, you're human. You can't haunt anyone." Still, he paused and gave her a second look.

Sophie just gave him a dark grin that made her freckles stand out even more than usual. "Every. Single. Day."

Mortimer shook his head. "Look, girls. I don't have time for all of this. The fairy council says I'm supposed to give you gifts, so here is your gift." He began to make little circles with his hands. "Eva of the once-farmers, I give you this gift for your generosity. Play your harp with fingers or bow, plants will wither or plants will grow. All that's needed is music and mood, whether your mood is bitter or good." And with that, he waved his hands in the air, throwing a sheet of sparks over Eva and disappearing into the afternoon sky.

~

"Alright, what's this about?" Rynn put down her broom and looked at Eva. The little hen house wasn't swept clean yet, but when Rynn wore that look of determination, nothing would deter her.

"What do you mean?" Eva kept her eyes on the basket as she gathered the eggs.

"You hate the chickens. You wouldn't be here unless . . ." Rynn quirked an eyebrow. "You're hiding from Mother and Father, aren't you?"

Eva simply kept gathering. "I've never disliked finding the eggs. It's the droppings I take issue with."

Rynn laughed. "Then I suppose you owe Mortimer a thank-you for removing us from the woods."

Eva shivered. She knew her sister was just trying to cheer her up, but she couldn't find it in herself to laugh.

Rynn nudged her and then put an arm around Eva's shoulders. "Hey, it could be worse. It's such an obscure gift . . ." She shrugged her shoulders. "Maybe no one will even notice."

Eva put down her basket and sighed. The chicken coop was certainly not her favorite place on the mansion grounds. The corners were too close, and that was just an invitation for spiders. And the smell was gut wrenching. The chickens themselves weren't so bad, as long as none of them decided to peck at an arm or fingers while one was gathering. And she was telling the truth about the eggs. The blue ones were her favorite.

She sighed again. Just like her beautiful dress.

"Eva, I know you're out here somewhere!" Sophie shouted. Eva cringed as her sister came stampeding through the door, nearly stepping on a chicken in the process.

"I've been looking everywhere for you! Why did you run off like that? Mortimer disappears and so do you! I thought at first that he'd taken you!"

"To avoid something like this," Eva muttered, but Sophie seemed in no mood to listen.

"Why didn't you fight it?"

"No need to get so worked up." Rynn put her hands on her hips. "Eva just needed some space. I knew that, and you should have, too."

"I wasn't talking to you, Rynn." Sophie glared at Eva.

Eva raised an eyebrow. "Really? You wanted me to *fight* Mortimer? He's a fairy!"

"He could use a good slugging, but that's not what I meant."

"Then what did you mean?"

Sophie put her hands on her hips and huffed. "You didn't even protest! You just took the gift as it was and took the low road, just like you always do!"

"Hold on, now!" Eva put her basket down. "I do *not* always take the low road!"

"You play it safe, and you let people run right over you."

"I—" Eva started, but Sophie shook her head emphatically.

"You did the same thing when Elizabeth White called you Lumber Man. Not once did you stand up for yourself. She only stopped when I started putting ants in her rouge."

Rynn opened her mouth, but whatever she was about to say was drowned out by the sound of their parents calling Eva's name outside. Eva looked up at Rynn. *Hide me,* she mouthed. But it was too late. Her parents were nearing the hen house. So she picked up her basket again and forced a smile on her face.

"Eva! Eva where—oh, there you are." Her mother stopped so fast in the doorway that her father ran right into her from behind. Eva and Rynn exchanged an amused glance as their parents glared at each other before jumping right back into whatever they had chased her down for.

"Eva," her mother waved a fistful of papers in the air, "would you like to explain to me why we have received marriage proposals from thirteen farmers, three florists, and a witch doctor?"

"Not that we're complaining, of course." Their father grinned. "All honest, hard-working stock these folks are." He grabbed the papers from his wife and thumbed through them before pulling one out. "Except for maybe this witch doctor fellow." He shuddered. "Never liked them." He looked up at his wife in confusion. "Who claimed to be a witch doctor? They don't even exist!"

"Some poor sap who wants to con people," Martin said.

"Martin's right. You shouldn't marry that one, Eva" Penny said.

Their mother briefly closed her eyes and shook her head. "For just a moment, let's forget *who* you have proposals from, and let's return to the question of just *why* you have been proposed to by *seventeen* men in one afternoon."

Rynn stepped forward. "It wasn't her fault—"

But Eva put a hand on her sister's arm and pulled her back. It took everything in her not to cringe visibly at what she knew her parents would say, or to cringe at the fact that her father was delighted with these sudden proposals, but the sooner she got this over with, the better.

"Do you . . ." She swallowed hard, as her voice suddenly fled her. "Do you remember that blue dress that you ordered for me?"

"Yes," her mother said. "Didn't you go with the girls to get that finished today? I meant to tell you I was hoping to see it." When Eva said nothing, she added slowly, "Where is it?"

Eva looked at her feet. If this had been any other family, she wouldn't be having this stupid conversation. What parents got upset when their children did something kind? In a small voice, she finally managed to squeak, "I might have given it away."

Her parents squinted at her then understanding dawned on their faces.

"Oh, Eva," her father groaned, "you didn't."

"Eva! You know better! Mortimer hasn't been around in over a year! What if he decided—" Then she put her hand over her heart. "Who did you give your dress to?"

"Elizabeth White," Eva mumbled.

Her father rubbed his chin with his hand. "Isn't she the one that—"

"Yes! Yes." Eva wanted to scream. "She called me Lumber Man the entire year I was ten because I was a skinny, shapeless beanpole who towered over everyone else. Now, can we please get on with this?"

Her mother stepped forward and took Eva by the shoulders. But this time, her eyes were sad and gentle. She placed a hand softly on Eva's cheek. "Did Mortimer visit you after you gave your dress away?"

Eva's eyes pricked, and all she could do was nod.

Her father drew in a deep breath and let it out slowly. "What did that blasted fairy do this time?"

Rynn made a face. "He's been experimenting again, and he got pretty creative. Even for him." She picked her broom up and attacked the floor with a vengeance.

"He . . ." Eva said softly. "He said that whenever I play the harp, depending on my mood, plants will either wither or grow." She closed her eyes and shook her head. "It didn't make sense."

"Well," her father scratched the back of his head, "I guess there's only one way to find out."

Soon everyone, including Eva's brother and sisters, were gathered in her room all around her harp. Eva sat down and bit her lip. Her father held a baby pumpkin plant in a pot.

"All right, Eva," her mother said. "Let's see what happens."

Trembling, Eva raised her fingers to the strings. But she couldn't bring herself to play.

"Pretend you're at the Winter Ball," Ellie offered kindly. "Pick one of the pieces you've been practicing."

Taking a deep breath, Eva nodded and straightened her shoulders. It didn't matter whether she played now or an hour later, the truth would come out somehow. And so she began to play.

About four lines into the song, her father let out a cry of dismay. "The pumpkin!"

Eva stopped playing and stood to see what everyone else was crowding around. There, in her father's pot, lay the baby pumpkin. Or what used to be a pumpkin, at least. Her stomach dropped as she examined the charred, crumbled remains of what had been a beautiful little squash.

"Father!" Her hands flew to her mouth. "I'm so sorry . . ." She looked up at her mother, who looked equally shocked, and then at her siblings.

"Didn't Mortimer say something about making plants grow?" Martin asked. "Maybe if you played something happier?"

Liesa huffed at her brother. "You weren't even there. How would you know?"

Martin scowled at his younger sister. "I listen more than you think I do."

"No," Eva said as she sat back down at her harp, "I think Martin's right. Or at least, I hope he is," she muttered, placing her fingers back on the instrument.

Which song should she play? But no, Mortimer hadn't said to play something happy. He had said her *mood* had to be good. For one brief moment, Eva wished she had smacked the fairy when she had the chance. Leave it to Mortimer to base magic on feelings instead of actions. They were so much harder to control. How in the blazes was she supposed to feel happy at a moment like this?

After a moment of thinking, she began to plug away at the harp again. Only this time, she kept her eyes closed. For when her eyes were closed, she wasn't sitting in her room, surrounded by her family after being cursed by the family's incompetent fairy godfather. Instead, she was at the Winter Ball, wearing her beautiful crystal-studded gown once more, and she was playing her music for the entire city, praying they would all feel the same way about the songs as she did.

"I don't see anything changing—" her mother was saying when Penny shrieked.

"Out the window! Look at Mother's rose outside the window!"

Eva stopped playing and turned to look out of the window by her bed. She gasped along with her family. Their mother's favorite yellow rose bush had climbed all the way up the sill and to the roof.

"Of course *that* had to be the one to grow," her father mumbled, but her mother only stared at Eva with a look of horror on her face. For a moment, no one said anything.

"I'm not marrying any of those suitors," Eva finally managed to squeak.

"They must have either seen or heard the story from people who were in the square, the same way I did," Martin said, glaring out the window at the rose bush. "They weren't interested until they thought she could make them rich." He turned to their parents. "You're not going to make Eva marry any of them," he paused, "are you?"

Their parents shared a look. As she often did, Eva wondered what they were saying in their silence.

Finally, her father slowly looked away from her mother and straight at Eva. "As much as your mother and I approve of the *kind* of fellows these gentlemen are . . . all except that witch doctor fellow . . . I'm afraid we can't let you be taken advantage of here."

Eva let out a deep breath of relief. "Thank you. Thank you so much!"

But her mother was already shaking her head. "In order to do that, I'm afraid you're going to have to leave."

"Leave?" Eva blanched. "You mean, as in . . . I have to move?" She looked around at her brother and sisters. "Away from all of you?"

Her mother's eyes were already filling with tears. And yet, she nodded.

"Immediately."

ONE YEAR LATER...

1

YOU STAY OUT OF THIS

*J*ack paused on the threshold of the big tavern and dusted himself off. He'd done his best to wash and air out his father's old trousers and what had been his favorite shirt, white with blue buttons, before the dance, but the long walk from his house to the tavern had made them all dirty again. Still, they were a far cry nicer than anything he had ever owned.

Two sets of footsteps ran up behind him.

"I made it first! You have to muck out the horse stalls tomorrow!" Jack could hear the smirk in the boy's voice.

"Did not! We tied!" A younger voice cried.

Jack turned to face his brothers. "Look at you! You're both filthy!" He knelt and tried to dust them off, too, but it was little use. "Did you look for every mud hole to splash in on the way?"

"If Mother would buy us new clothes, it would be easier to stay clean," Larry grumbled.

"Well, she isn't going to do that anytime soon, so you'd do best to try and keep clean what you have," Jack replied, running his fingers through their fine blond hair in vain attempts to comb it.

"If she worked more instead of staying inside all day, we'd get to go to more fun nights like this," Ray added with a scowl.

"None of that now. We should just be grateful she let us go out tonight. While we're here, we're going to have fun and not think dreary thoughts like that. Yes?" He did his best to put on a convincing smile. When they nodded, he gave them each a playful shove and led them inside.

The tavern was already abuzz with people, drinking and laughing and dancing. Older women and young mothers stood in one corner and gossiped as they watched their children play, while most of the men stood over by the bar and drank ale.

"There's Reddick!" Larry pointed. "Can we go?"

"Just stay in the tavern. No sneaking out for pranks. And Ray, mind Larry. Do what he says."

"Aw, do I have to?"

"He's older. Now go play."

As soon as his brothers were with their friends, Jack turned to search for his own friends among those drinking ale. Sure enough, he spotted two men waving him over.

"Well, look who finally showed up!" Johnathon slapped him on the back as Jack raised his hand for a mug and then leaned back against the counter.

"It hasn't been that long. I came two months ago."

"No," Kayden shook his head and took a drink. "You haven't been to one of these since last winter. I remember because we'd just had that big freeze."

Jack nodded in thanks to the tavern keep as he took his mug. "Whatever the time, it's good to be back." He studied the people in attendance. "I see a few new faces. But where's Aaron?"

"Wow," Johnathon shook his head, his red hair shining in the light of the wooden chandeliers above, "you have been gone a long time."

"I'm not gone. Just busy."

Johnathon shrugged. "He left early last spring for the university in Tulkarnie."

Jack nodded and swigged some ale, hoping his disappointment wasn't written all over his face. Unfortunately, his friends had known him too long to be fooled.

"You could go, too, you know," Kayden said, his dark eyes intense. But then they were always that way. The man could talk about corn and look excited. "He's only two years your junior, and you were always smarter than him."

"With what money?" Jack asked, surveying the room again. Anything to avoid looking his friends in the eyes.

Johnathon hailed the tavern keep for another round. "I've heard some of the universities are always looking for unexpected students, people they can educate and shove at their kings as advisers. It makes the crown more likely to pay for the university's expenses. Or something like that."

Jack shrugged. "I appreciate your confidence, but they wouldn't want a backwards farmer from middle-of-nowhere Guthward."

"You never know until you try." Kayden peered up at him more closely, his bright eyes searching Jack's face. "But we all know that's not the reason you won't go."

"He's right," Johnathon said. "You're twenty and one years! How long are you going to let her run your life?"

"As long as she owns the deed to the land." Jack put his mug down just a little too hard on the counter. It clinked loudly, gaining him a quick glare from the tavern keep. "If I left, Larry and Ray would have to run the whole blasted farm themselves. And Larry won't even be ten for another six months."

"You could always take them with you. Let your mother run that piece of garbage on her own for a while. It would do her some good to work, instead of letting you do everything around there," Kayden said.

"He's right," Johnathon added. "Besides, you've talked about having a family one day. What self-respecting woman in her right mind is going to marry you when your *mother* is still telling you what to do?"

"Look," Jack said, downing the rest of his ale in one swallow, "can we not talk about this? I came here to have a good time tonight." As he spoke, a flash of gold caught his eye, and though he knew it was rude, Jack couldn't help staring.

He'd seen the young woman numerous times throughout the year at town-hall gatherings, the market, and even at a few berry-picking parties. She lived with her cousin, Tamra, and her husband and children in their farmhouse on the other side of town. He'd been trying to work up the courage to speak to her, as she was one of the few young women who hadn't grown up with him and probably wasn't aware of the war he and his mother had been waging for almost a decade, but every time he went to speak with her, she was called away, usually to watch her cousin's children. And from what he could see, this night was no different.

"What are you waiting for? If you want to dance with her, just go over and ask her." Jonathan gave him a shove. He gave Jack an evil grin. "She doesn't know your mother. You might stand half a chance."

But Kayden shook his head. "Don't do it, Jack. That girl may be beautiful, but I hear that her family is even stranger than yours." He nodded in the girl's direction. "That's why she's living with her cousin's family."

Jack turned to study the girl from across the room again. He still couldn't believe that no one had asked her onto the dance floor. Her thick golden hair flowed down her shoulders like a waterfall of sunlight, and her dark eyes were wide and innocent. Of course, this summer festival was the first town dance that he'd been able to attend all year. Perhaps other men had asked her at prior celebrations and found her to be boring, or maybe she'd stepped on their toes. But the longer he watched her, the more he doubted those possibilities. She was unusually tall, but surprisingly, her height only seemed to add to her allure, making her look long and graceful, like one of the willow trees that grew around the creek. Whenever she moved, she seemed lithe, her movements confident and sure, and judging by the gentle smile that would light her face every now and then, she looked to be anything but dull.

Jack folded his arms across his chest. "It's not odd to be living with a relative, particularly when you're a girl of her age. She's what, eighteen? Nineteen?"

"Eighteen. But it doesn't matter." Kayden frowned. "When your relatives are Tamra and Davies, living with them is *very* odd. Those two make your old lady look like a fairy godmother who flies around all day and grants wishes."

Jack handed the mug back to the tavern keep. "Well then, it shouldn't be too difficult to sweep her off her feet." He turned and gave his friends a bow. "Now, if you scoundrels can bear to part with me, I have some wooing to do."

"Good luck," Kayden said doubtfully.

As he crossed the room, dodging children and stepping carefully around the open floor full of couples twirling to the musicians' tunes, the girl turned toward him, and he found himself staring into the biggest golden-brown eyes he'd ever seen. For a long moment, they stayed that way, Jack rooted to his spot on the edge of the dance floor. But then, her lips were suddenly mashed together tightly, and those beautiful brown eyes grew fierce. She stood abruptly and marched away.

Jack tried to ignore the laughing he could hear coming from his friends behind him. What had happened? Had she not wanted to speak with him? Jack took a moment and tried to remember doing anything that might have offended her. They'd never actually spoken before, but she had to at least recognize him. Again, he regretted not attending more of the recent village dances.

Just as he was about to return in shame to his friends, however, he spotted her walking quickly over to a corner where the children were playing. Jack followed at a distance, watching as she looked around for a moment before darting into a crowded corner and then reemerging a moment later with a small child in her arms.

As he got closer, he could see that the squirming little girl she carried appeared to be quite . . . naked. He tried to smother a chuckle as he spotted the toddler's missing dress crumpled under a nearby window. He went and retrieved it.

"Looking for something?" He held out the little girl's dress.

The young woman stared at him blankly for a moment before relief flooded her face and she grabbed the dress from his hands. In one smooth motion, she'd wrestled the wriggling child into a sitting position and had the dress back on in less than a minute. Once the little girl was dressed again, she let the child go, turned to him, and sighed.

"I can't tell you how grateful I am. I wasn't sure where she put it, and my cousin would be more than put out with me if I . . ." She stopped and pursed her lips. "I'm sorry. I'm rambling. Thank you so much, Mr. . . ." She tilted her head and raised her eyebrows.

"Oh, just call me Jack. That's what everyone else does." He knelt down beside the toddler, who was now beginning to kick and scream again. "You want to see something?"

The toddler continued to protest, not even giving him a second glance until he pulled a bright red handkerchief from his pocket and held it in front of her face. When he'd caught her attention, he folded it carefully into his sleeve. Then he whipped out a small pink sugar candy in its place and handed it to the little girl.

She took the candy in her little chubby hands and stared at him in awe before hopping up and screaming for her mommy to look at her gift.

The young woman turned to him. "Well, I'm impressed. Most men wouldn't get within twenty feet of a screaming child if they could help it. But your timing is impeccable." Her brown eyes sparkled as they swept over him. When she smiled, he noticed that her right cheek had a dimple while her left had none.

Jack nodded to Ray and Larry, who were in another corner with the older children. "It's always good to be prepared. Those two keep me on my toes, so I've learned never to be without some sort of bribe."

Immediately, a guarded look swept her face, and the bright curiosity that had been there moments before was gone. To his disappointment, polite interest took its place.

"Oh," her voice was distant, "so those are your children."

Jack stared at her blankly until understanding dawned on him. "Oh! Oh, no, no, no." He felt his cheeks turn red as he laughed in embarrassment, running his hand through his hair. "No, those are my brothers. Ray! Larry! Come here and meet . . ." He realized he still didn't know her name.

"Eva." She tucked a tendril of blonde hair behind her ear. "My name is Eva." Then she knelt to meet his brothers eye-to-eye. "It's nice to meet you both. How old are you?"

Jack couldn't help but watch in awe. Usually, the few girls that he'd ever made any sort of progress with in the past had taken off the moment they discovered that he was practically a full-time nanny to his siblings. But judging by the grateful smile on her face when he had produced the candy, and the seemingly genuine interest she was now showing in his brothers, Jack couldn't help but wonder if this girl just might be different.

"They're sweet," she said as they scampered away. Then her grin fell a little.

"What's wrong?" He instinctively stepped closer.

She gave him a sad smile. "Oh, nothing. Well, that's not true, either. I suppose I miss my family."

"I take it you have a big one?"

She laughed, the sound like the song of a robin. "You could say that. After my sister, Rynn, I'm the second oldest. Then comes Sophie, then the twins, Martin and Elisette. Then the other twins, Anneliese and Penny." She smiled again, more to herself, it seemed, than him, but it was pretty just the same. "It's not talked about, but I think we all knew my parents never meant to have quite so many children. I always liked it, though. We took care of each other." She wrapped her arms around herself and hunched over a little bit. Despite the girl's impressive height, as she was nearly as tall as Jack, the posture made her look vulnerable. Jack decided that this bothered him more than he would have expected.

"So," he looked back and forth between Eva and the dance floor and wondered how to close the gap in-between, "I suspect you watch your younger cousins quite often?" What was wrong with him? Couldn't he make better conversation than that?

To his surprise, however, her smile became tight-lipped, and her brown eyes gained a fire to them. "Every single day," she said, enunciating every word with disgust.

Now his interest was truly piqued.

"And that's not what you wanted?"

Eva sighed and closed her eyes. "It's not so much that I dislike my cousins, because I don't." She looked at the dancers wistfully as they spun around in the center of the floor. "I suppose it's more that I never imagined myself here in this place. I do what I'm told day in and day out, and there's never an end in sight. I'm stuck." The more she talked, the harder she glared in the direction of where her cousins were sitting, chatting happily away with their neighbors.

How did one respond to that? Jack found himself more than curious about what kind of situation could have driven Eva away from the family she loved so much, when he remembered what Kayden had said about her family being strange. Was this why none of his peers or even the older single men had been actively seeking this girl? Because they were afraid of her past?

"I've been here nearly a year," she said in a louder voice, as though trying to distract him from their present conversation, "but this is the first dance I've been to. Tamra's always kept me at home. What exactly is it?" She paused before laughing and adding, "And why are we in a tavern?"

"Sulta Springs is a farming town through and through," Jack

said, "but we enjoy a little fun here and there. So we try to see how many community events we can fit in during the year. This particular dance is held once a month. And we hold it in the tavern because it's the biggest building in town." But not to be deterred, he pitched his voice a little lower. "Going back to what we were talking about earlier, I hope you don't mind me asking, but were you in danger of any kind back with your family?"

Eva shook her head, wearing a slight frown. "Not directly. I suppose you could say—"

"Eva!"

Jack and Eva both turned around to see Eva's cousin, Tamra, leading a well-dressed gentleman behind her. Jack didn't miss the little sigh that escaped Eva as she donned what looked like a false grin where she had been thoughtful just a moment before. But before her cousin arrived at their sides, she leaned over toward him and whispered, "Thank you so much for talking with me tonight. I've really enjoyed it. Truly."

"Eva, I've been looking everywhere for you." Tamra and the gentleman stopped in front of them. Then Tamra turned an unimpressed eye upon Jack. "Hello, Jack." She sounded about as enthusiastic as a cat preparing for its bath. "I hope your mother is better."

"As well as she'll ever be." It was Jack's turn this time to grow rigid. How Eva put up living with Tamra and Davies for an entire year without losing her mind, Jack would never understand.

"Well," Tamra gave a sly grin and hooked her arm around the gentleman's elbow. "It seemed she let you out tonight at least."

Jack bristled. "I let myself out."

"I'm sure you did. Now, if you'll excuse me, Duke Carlton here was asking about Eva. Duke, this is my younger cousin Eva."

The gentleman, who looked to be just a few years older than Jack, and had an uncanny resemblance to a pigeon, bowed low and took Eva's hand. Bringing it to his lips, he kissed it. The kiss wasn't quick though, and after several seconds, became the most awkward greeting Jack had ever seen. He shifted uncomfortably as Eva's eyes flickered to his and then back down to her hand. Just as Jack was considering saying something—anything—to distract the duke, the man himself stood and grinned, not letting go of her fingers.

"My dear, my name is Duke Carlton Rafael Sebastian the Third. I am the Duke of Monte David."

"I am honored to meet you." Eva kept her eyes away from his but made a slight curtsey.

"He owns the land west of town." Tamra's gray eyes gleamed as she looked at Eva. Jack could tell he was being dismissed. He took a few steps back but refused to retreat to the other side of the room. Not just yet. He could already see that the duke was sizing Eva up. As though the flabby little man had any right to judge another based on looks. *He* looked as though he hadn't seen a day of hard work in his life.

And Jack didn't like it.

"I am told by your most gracious cousin," the duke began, "that you are from Astoria. Though I was born here in Guthward, I had the supreme privilege of attending the university in Astoria, and was of no small consequence there myself as I became purposefully familiar with your systems of magic and general familiarity with fairies and other sorts of inhuman creatures." He took a step forward, to which Eva responded by taking a step back. Jack wanted badly to laugh. He wasn't sure why, but this made him feel somewhat triumphant. He might not be a duke, but she hadn't backed away from him.

"Eva, why didn't you ever tell us that you play the harp?" Tamra said in a loud voice. "A whole year of living with us, and you haven't once sat down to the instrument."

Eva's face went completely white, and for a moment Jack was afraid she might pass out then and there. "Where did you hear that?" she whispered.

"The duke apparently had the high privilege of hearing your name over and over again in the music community in Astoria."

Tamra fairly glowed, her usually pink cheeks nearly the color of strawberries.

"Indeed," the duke said. "I cannot play myself, but I consider myself quite a student of music. Particularly," he looked straight at Eva, "the harp."

If Eva had looked wary at the duke's introduction, she looked downright terrified at these words.

"I was hoping," the duke continued, seeming completely unaware of Eva's discomfort, "that I might have the vast honor of hearing you play tonight."

"I . . . I don't think that would be a wise idea," Eva stammered.

"Eva," her cousin bristled, "Duke Carlton is our better. If King Eston doesn't sire a child before he dies, Duke Carlton will inherit the throne. And he has just done the honor of asking you to play." She turned and pointed at the instruments in the corner of the room where the musicians were taking a brief rest. "I want you to go up there and play. Now."

Jack couldn't stand it any longer. Duke or not, this was not acceptable.

"If Eva doesn't want to play," Jack fixed Tamra with his fiercest glare, then the duke, "then she doesn't have to. There is no law—"

"You stay out of this, farm boy!" Tamra pointed a finger in Jack's face.

The duke held up his hands. Jack couldn't help noticing how soft and round they were. A good indication of his kind of work. "No, the boy is right. I've seen all I need to see." He bowed to Eva and nodded once at Jack, a strange small smile crossing his face as his gaze rested finally on Eva. "Enjoy the rest of the party." And then he walked away.

Tamra threw a livid glance at Eva before following the duke, apologizing profusely as she went. Only when they were gone did Jack realize that Eva was gripping his arm.

He turned to her, all thoughts of fun aside. When he spoke, it was in a low voice that he hoped their neighbors couldn't hear. "Are you well?"

Eva stared at the duke's retreating back until it was lost in the crowd, and even after that, several long seconds passed before she tore her gaze away and met Jack's eyes.

"I'm not sure." Then she seemed to recover herself, removing her hands from his arm and taking a step back. Jack found that this disappointed him. He couldn't explain why, but a voice inside insisted this girl needed help. He just wished she would tell him what was frightening her so.

"You can tell me," he said softly. "I want to help if I can." He let out a small laugh and rubbed his head. "It's just hard to do that when I don't know what you need help with."

Her eyes lost their panicked shine, and finally a small smile appeared. "I believe you," she said. Then the frightened look returned. "Unfortunately, this is something I need to do alone right now." She looked at the window and then back at him. "Will you be here when I get back?"

He nodded. "If you think that would be best, but I—"

"Thank you!" And with that, she hurried toward the door, her skirts billowing behind her as she fled.

2

WE ARE FALLING MADLY IN LOVE

*E*va left the crowded party and turned the nearest corner. Only when she was sure that neither Jack nor her cousin nor anyone else was following her, did she stop and press herself up against the town hall's wall and look up to the sky.

"Mortimer!" she hissed. "I need you!"

The night stayed silent. Not even the clouds moved past the moon. She glanced over her shoulder and tried again.

"I don't have time to do your silly chant! Please, I'm in danger! I know you can hear me!"

Three sets of heavy footsteps sounded around the corner.

Eva looked back up at the sky, her heart racing as she tried to remember the chant. All the woodcutter's children knew it, but she'd never actually used it before.

"Oh great and . . ." Wait. Was it *great and powerful* or just—

A hand clamped over her mouth. Eva tried to scream, but her mouth was gagged, her eyes were covered with a blindfold, and her wrists and ankles were bound. Still, she tried to kick and fight her way free as she was lifted by a thick pair of arms that smelled like sweat and soil.

As she was dragged across the gravel, she wished with all her heart that Jack had ignored her wishes and followed her out. Hope-fully, he wouldn't try to take three men on his own. He was strong enough for sure to take on one, maybe two. Though Tamra's husband was decently muscled, the width of Jack's shoulders put him to shame. Still, strong or not, she would hate it if Jack were injured on her account. Perhaps, though, he could at least sound the alarm or go get help.

But by the time they had dragged her across the gravel, there was still no sign of Jack's messy blond hair or his friendly gray eyes. There was no sign of anything, as she tried desperately, and unsuc-cessfully, to remove her blindfold. She despaired as her captor placed her on some sort of wobbly seat, and the wobbly seat began to bounce up and down. In her attempt to prevent anyone from discovering her secret, she'd prepared the way for the very people, it seemed, who did know.

∼

The soft cushioned seats and the lack of wind made Eva think she was in a carriage, but without being able to see shadows or the direction of the moon, it was difficult to tell how long they traveled or how far. Every few minutes, Eva would get up the nerve to try and loosen her bonds. But there were too many, and they were all too tight.

What a waste. The entire year had been a big fat waste. Her parents had sent her away to her awful cousin who had absolutely no interest in her own children, in a kingdom that had nothing but hills and hills of rolling red clay dirt and sometimes tornados, with nothing to show for it but her abduction. She might as well have stayed in Astoria. At least her siblings would have made the kidnapping a challenge.

The carriage finally came to a stop. No words were exchanged between her kidnappers, but someone opened the door with a click, and the one that smelled like sweat lifted her again and gently carried her out. He didn't set her down, though, until he had crossed a wide expanse outside and then moved into the warmth of the indoors. Even there, he continued to carry her up several flights of stairs and through a number of turns, until she was finally placed in a chair. When her blindfold was removed and her legs unbound, she blinked in the bright light of countless candles set all about in a very large room. And across from her, in a chair of his own, sat the duke.

"Hello, Miss Eva. Welcome to Monte David." He stood and gave her a short bow before sitting again and pouring himself a cup of tea. Then he poured a second. "Cream?"

Eva watched him warily. She'd thought him odd at the party, but now she could see that he was stark raving mad. He had to be. No sane man would kidnap a girl and then offer her tea.

"You really ought to try the cream," he said when she didn't reply. "Here, I'll show you." He began to pour a thick stream of white liquid into her cup.

She probably should have been more watchful of what he was putting in her tea, but as her eyes adjusted to the brightness, she couldn't help being distracted by the sheer opulence of the room.

The room itself was three times the size of the one she'd occupied back in their mansion in Astoria, with balconies on opposite sides, a bed larger than she'd ever seen before, not one but two vanities, and random couches and chairs and tables scattered about the room. There were three chandeliers hanging from the ceiling, and everything was covered in either gold or silver. On the vanities were spread a vast assortment of jewels, silver, and gold in a wide array of rings, bracelets, necklaces, and earrings. What caught her attention most, however, were the two harps, one on each balcony.

The harp on the balcony that faced the mountain was silver. From her seat inside, she could see that its column, crown, and neck were covered with rubies of every shape and size. And though the other harp was farther away on the other balcony, she could see that it was gold, and she was fairly certain that it was covered in emeralds.

" . . . if you can see the bottom of the teacup, there's not enough cream. But if you cannot see past the surface of the tea when you place a spoon inside," the duke said, fastidiously studying his cup as he demonstrated, "then you have too much." He looked up at Eva, a brilliant smile on his face. However, it melted quickly. "My dear, are you listening?"

Eva slowly shook her head. "What is this place?" Then she looked at him directly. "Why am I here?"

"Eva," he took her hands in his.

She would have yanked them out, except for the fact that she was still bound at the wrists.

"I have just explained and shown you an example of how to pour the perfect amount of cream. If you can't listen to something as simple as—"

"I know how to pour tea."

"Yes, but if you would just watch—"

"Sir!" Eva did her best to yank her hands back. "My family may have been woodcutters once, but I was trained by the most sought-after governess in all of Astoria. I know *exactly* how to pour cream. What I *want* to know is why you kidnapped me and what I'm doing here."

Though she hadn't found him particularly attractive at the party, Eva now noticed how annoyingly round the duke's head was as he nodded sympathetically in response to her questions. His ears were also around, as was his midsection, particularly so for a man of his age, which she guessed to be about twenty and five. The only thing about the duke that didn't seem well rounded was his ability to think. That seemed to go in only one direction.

He stood and put his hands behind his back. "When your most excellent cousin introduced us at the dance, I believe she mentioned that I am next in line for the Guthwardian crown. Meaning, if King Eston cannot find a suitable wife and produce an heir, the throne will fall to me." He turned and fixed her with a steady gaze.

Eva watched him for a moment before she realized he was expecting a response. The words on the tip of her tongue were not appropriate for a lady to use, so she stayed silent and waited for him to go on.

Still, he kept his gaze steady. "Does that not impress you?"

Eva felt her jaw drop. Was he in earnest? "Sir, you have abducted me against my will. Nothing you say is going to impress me."

He gave a start, his eyes wide as though this surprised him. Finally, he began again. "Being raised in such a forward-thinking and modern kingdom as Astoria, you may not be aware that not all kingdoms are as *civilized* as yours. I don't know if you know this, but the thick red clay that my countrymen call soil might be good for agriculture, but it inhibits most use of magic."

Despite her resolve to remain unmoved, Eva did find herself a bit curious at this. She had wondered over the past year at the lack of fairies or any sign of their existence, so his explanation about the soil made sense. Not that she had missed the magic at all.

"Even more infuriating is the fact that our king and people seem completely at ease with the shortfall. Against it, even! I've told my cousin that there are ways to remedy the soil shortcoming if only people are willing to take advantage of them. But with most of our people content with their lot as farmers and millers and all sorts of common rabble, convincing anyone that we need magic has been a nearly hopeless cause." He paused to take a sip of tea. As he did, Eva tried not to let him see that she had finally managed to loosen one of her wrist bindings. To her relief, as soon as he was done swallowing, which was a rather loud process, he continued, hardly glancing her way.

"Though I was never content with Guthward's contentedness, I, too, was unaware as to just how far behind the rest of the world we had fallen. Until . . ." his green eyes took on a dreamy look, "I went to the university in Astoria."

Eva wanted to gag. He looked as though he might break into song.

"It was there that I learned just how much magic had to offer. I attended classes on trolls and fairies and even more minute details such as fairy gifts and wishes, and the magic objects they bestow."

"What were you studying?" Eva asked.

"Economics."

"And you were studying magic?"

"The university's library had a large selection of books on the subject, so it isn't that odd. Anyhow, that's beside the point!"

"You tried to get a fairy godparent, didn't you? But you were rejected." Eva smirked.

Her abductor looked slightly ruffled. "The longer I studied, the more I realized the danger my kingdom was in. It would be nothing for another kingdom to gather some fairies and swoop in and take us in our sleep, completely unaware."

"Apparently, you have very little experience with fairies." Her family could barely manage one, let alone an army.

"So as soon as I was finished with my studies, I went straight to my cousin and described to him exactly what we needed to do to fortify our borders."

"I take it that he paid you no heed?"

"He laughed at me! Even when I described to him all the grotesque ways we might be overrun by trolls, he only waved my fears aside. 'We've lived this way since Guthward become its own kingdom,' he said. 'No reason to upset folks when magic is barely usable here.'"

Eva sighed. Despite her earlier success with the rope on her right wrist, the one on her left refused to budge. "I still don't see what any of this has to do with me."

He knelt beside her. His breath smelled like old cheese. "I was also in Astoria when you were bestowed with such a wonderful gift! I heard about you, and immediately, it was clear that you were destined to be mine!" His voice dropped to a whisper. "You and I are going to be in Guthwardian history books from now on." He leaned in closer and whispered, breathing all over her face in the process. "We're going to bring magic to our kingdom, and doing thus, we shall save it from future disaster!"

Eva tried to lean back. "But what can I—"

"Your gift, Eva! Your gift!"

Eva tried not to show how terrified she was fast becoming. "You don't even know me," she whispered. "You don't know what I can do."

At this, the stubby man beamed before pulling out a ledger from beneath his cloak. Opening it, he pointed with his finger to the top of the page so she could see. "Eva," he read, "second daughter of woodcutters in Astoria. Assigned a fairy godfather. Gifted by fairy godfather, can make plants grow or wither," he looked up, "by playing the harp."

Eva stared in horror. "You keep records on me?"

He snapped it shut. "See how much you mean to me already? I don't keep records on just anybody." When Eva couldn't bring herself to respond, he reopened the ledger and perused it until he stopped and nodded to himself. "Quite right. Eva, darling, we shall rest tonight, but tomorrow we will begin."

"Begin what?"

He walked over to the silver harp on the west balcony facing the mountain. "Every evening, you will play a bitter song on the harp facing the mountain. Every morning, you'll begin by playing a sweet song on the harp facing east."

Eva glanced back at the mountain range through the west balcony. Though she couldn't see well from where she was sitting, the mountains, which were flat and hardly tall enough to be considered real mountains, seemed to end right behind the house or whatever it was that she was in. On the east side, there were no mountains. Only rolling hills as far as she could see in the moonlight.

"Why?" She narrowed her eyes. "What are we killing?"

"Don't worry so much about what you'll be killing. Think of it as creating open land to grow beans to keep the entire kingdom fed!"

She shook her head. "I'm not growing or killing anything for you."

He froze, looking confused. "But if you don't, I'll have to punish your family. And that would make everything just awkward. Please don't make me do that, Eva."

Eva drooped in her chair, suddenly exhausted. She had just spent the last several hours racking her brains, trying to come up with some way to get away. And with just a few words, he had dashed every hope she had of escape.

"My dear!" He rushed to her side and knelt to the ground. "Don't look so sad!" His eyes were suddenly bright, glistening with unshed tears. "It is all for the good of Guthward as a whole. I promise! Now . . . now if you'll just . . . if you'll just look around." He gestured to the room around them. "Everything you see in here is yours. I tried to imagine everything a young woman might desire. You have every jewel of the rainbow on your vanities over there, and I have an extensive library in my study that you may visit if you wish. And . . . and here!" He bounded over to the large golden wardrobe standing against one of the walls. Throwing it open, he revealed dozens of dresses. "Every single one of these is yours!"

Through the tears that burned her eyes, Eva glared at him and the dresses. "Why are they all green?"

He beamed. "I like green."

Eva rolled her eyes as he ran over to the far corner and pulled on a tassel that hung from the ceiling.

Two minutes later, a knock sounded at the door. He dashed over to open it and revealed a woman who looked to be in her fifth decade, holding a silver tray of pastries.

"This is Mrs. McConnell," he said. "She's my head housekeeper and can bring you anything your heart desires."

"I want to be free," Eva said, her voice shaking treacherously.

"People like *you* are the reason my family sent me to this awful place."

Making gentle shushing sounds, he knelt in front of her again and wiped the tears from her face with his thumbs. His hands were clammy. He laughed a little, as though he had any right to see humor in the situation. "Well, what do you know? My hands are all sweaty. You know, they say that the more you love someone, the more they make your hands sweat." He smiled sweetly. "Isn't that romantic?"

"No, that's disgusting." Through her tears, Eva stared at him, unsure whether her disgust or her horror was currently greater.

Mrs. McConnell briefly closed her eyes and shook her head. Eva didn't blame her. She couldn't imagine how awful it must be to have a master such as the duke. Unfortunately, she got the feeling she was about to find out.

The duke, meanwhile, had gone back to his ledger. Opening it up, he thumbed through it until another grin spread across his face. He cleared his throat and began to speak.

"I walked upon a dirty road.

I almost stepped upon a toad.

Such revelation made me sigh,

for I was all alone in life.

Just like the little slimy thing,

I had no one to make me sing."

Eva sent a desperate look to the housekeeper, who simply continued to shake her head and purse her lips tightly shut.

"I dreamed of finding a girl of beauty

who's small in frame, sees love as duty,

soft in form with eyes of blue.

Yours are not, but I suppose they'll do.

When our children come to be,

maybe they'll look a lot like me.

It would be such a pity

if they—"

"Children?" Eva shuddered. "Duke, I thought you wanted me to make plants grow or die or something of that nature. Whatever do you mean about children?"

"My dear Eva." He put the letter down and put his moist hands on her face. His round eyes were even wider than usual, making him appear surprised. "I thought you knew."

Eva shook her head emphatically.

He only held her face more tightly. "We are falling madly in love."

Eva threw up.

3

THAT'S NOT HOW THIS WORKS

*T*hree weeks. It had been three whole weeks since the town dance, and only now was Jack feeling well enough to escape his house for the first time since then. His mother claimed that it was only the ague and that Jack was lazy for not venturing out sooner, but Jack wasn't entirely sure that Tamra hadn't slipped some poison into his butter truffles in retaliation for speaking with Eva. After all, Eva had never come back after she ran outside, and when he'd asked Tamra about her, all he'd gotten was a scowl and a sharp reminder to mind his own business.

He hoped Eva was all right.

He also hoped he'd get to see her again soon. But hours after returning home from the dance, Jack had fallen so ill that he'd been unable to walk and barely able to eat. And though he had very little recollection of the time he spent tossing and turning on his straw mattress, after being forced to stay inside with his mother Jack was ready to go just about anywhere. Unfortunately, he wasn't prepared for the strange errand his mother gave him that morning after he stumbled into the kitchen for the first time in three weeks.

He stared at her in disbelief. "My ears must still be ringing from the fever. I thought you said you wanted me to *sell* the cow?"

"You're not ill anymore, so I can only assume you're just stupid and deaf. Yes, I want you to sell the cow. She's run dry since the crops quit growing."

Jack folded his arms across his chest. "I told you before, crops don't just stop growing." He fixed her with a knowing eye. "They will, however, stop growing if you forget to tend to them."

"Unlike you and your good-for-nothing father," she sneered, tossing her gray-streaked red hair with a sniff, "I've never been one to shirk my duties."

Jack wanted to snort at this, but he knew the only thing it would get him would be a cuff to the ear. So he swallowed the words that he wanted to say and instead asked to see the cow.

"She's out in the garden. Your brothers got her that far, but they couldn't make her budge after that."

"Ruining all your vegetables, I'm sure." Jack shook his head with a smug smile.

But his mother didn't smile back. "I told you, there are no vegetables to ruin! Now get the abominable cow and go sell her before we all die of starvation!"

"Yes, Mother." Jack let out a deep breath and went to do as he had been told. For not the first time, he wondered how long a man of his age could expect to respect his mother without being required to obey her every ridiculous whim.

Of course, it didn't help that she technically owned the land he and his brothers lived on as well. She had threatened to kick him off before, and she probably would have, had he not been the only one to work the farm.

"Ray! Larry! Where's the cow?" He made his way out into the bright sunlight, blinking as he stepped outside. As soon as his eyes adjusted, he spotted two blond mops of hair in the part of the garden where the rutabagas should have been. As he drew closer, however, he noted with surprise that his mother had been right about the garden. Every single piece of vegetation had withered and was slumped against the ground. As he stared in horrified wonder at what had been his mother's most prized possession, his little brothers came running up to him.

"What do you think?" Larry asked, his blue eyes shining and his mouth turned up in a mischievous curve. "It's amazing, isn't it?"

"It was amazing," Ray muttered, "until we ran out of food." He glared back at the garden with the unforgiving stare of a boy who was always hungry.

Jack scratched the back of his neck. "When did this start?"

Larry was fairly bouncing. "The day you got sick! Everything was normal when evening fell, and then the strange music came from across the plains—"

"Strange music?" Jack looked out over the rolling hills that surrounded them. "I thought that was my fevered imagination."

"Nope." Ray shook his head. "It happens every night, just after sunset."

Jack studied the fields a little more carefully. He was too far away to see every part of their farm, for the barn stood between him and most of the crops, but the part that he could see did not look promising. "Mother wants me to sell the cow, so we'll figure this out later. You want to come along?"

Larry immediately whooped and hollered as he tore off toward the road, but Ray frowned even harder. "She wants you to sell the cow? That milk is all we've had for the last three days. That and those wrinkled old apples from the back of the barn. And cooked oats. So many oats. He visibly shuddered. "I hate oats."

Jack shrugged. "You know Mother. When she gets an idea—"

"She only says the cow is dry because the Douglas's cow *did* run dry, and she can't stand to be shown up by someone who has it harder than her."

Jack thumped his skinny little brother on the back, grabbed a rope from the porch, and put it around the poor cow's neck. Then he began walking in the direction Larry had gone. "True though that may be, it's her cow, and we have to do as she says. Might as well make the best of it."

Despite the way his legs felt like jelly after five minutes of walking, and the way the movement made his head swim, Jack found the outing to be rather pleasant. At this time of day, he was usually hard at work in the fields. But his fever had only broken the night before, and he hadn't awakened until long after the sun had risen, much to his mother's dismay. No wonder the crops were dying. She hadn't seen fit to step foot outside that ridiculous garden in the three weeks he'd been sick. Not that he would have expected her to.

As they continued walking, however, the uneasy feeling returned as Jack realized that his wasn't the only farm that looked unhealthy. As they passed their neighbors' gardens and farms, each one was the same. Shriveled brown plants lay flat against the ground, contrasting with the bright red clay beneath. By the time they reached town, Jack was tempted to see if he could sneak the cow back into the barn and hide her there, hoping his mother would eventually forgive him for disobeying her when milk was all they had left.

But then, what would they feed it? According to Ray, they'd eaten nearly all the oats he'd set aside to feed the horses in the winter, and they'd been feeding the cow and horses all the hay set aside for the cow.

He paused at the edge of the auction platform where a small crowd of unhappy people had gathered to wait for the next auction. They were mostly strangers, which was unusual for his sleepy little town, and the way they eyed his cow set him on edge. So instead of going straight to the auctioneer, he decided to wait for the auction to begin, and he headed instead over to the drinking trough where he knew he would find some more trustworthy friends.

"The dead lives!" Jim Farnsworth greeted him as he approached the trough.

"Ray! Larry! You can visit the Millers, but don't leave their yard." He eyed the strange crowd across the street again before he turned back to shake hands with Jim and Robert. Jim looked a bit leaner than Jack remembered seeing him last, and Robert looked exhausted, but both gave him a hearty handshake and their usual smiles. Jack leaned in a bit closer. "What's going on around here?"

Jim gestured at the auction block. "People are packing up and moving out. Everyone else around here is waiting to buy their beans."

"Beans?" Jack asked.

"That's right. Beans. Soybeans are the only crop that's grown since this famine started."

"Mine are dead."

"So are everyone else's." Jim leaned forward, a gleam in his eye. "Word has it that that duke, the one that lives not too far west of here, has brought some sort of magic with him from Astoria that is keeping his crops alive." He leaned back and stretched. "And with him being the smart politician he is and all . . . I mean, the *kind soul* he is, rather," Jim smiled wryly, "he's been sending enough beans all over the place to keep folks alive. So those who don't want beans leave. Those who want to stay, buy."

"How far does the famine go?" Jack asked.

Robert looked at the inside of his mug. "All the way to the borders is what we're hearing."

Jack shook his head in disbelief. "Just three weeks. That's all it took?"

"Evidently." Jim frowned at Jack's cow. "What are you doing with old Sacha here? Better be careful, or you're going to get mugged as soon as you step out of town. Won't do for your brothers to see you all mashed up and bloodied."

"Too bad your father isn't here," Jim said with a grim smile. "That man knew how to fight, that's for sure." He made a face at Jack. "Not like those two hooligans you like to waste your time with. What were their names? Cayman and Paul?"

Jack gave his father's old friends a wry smile. "Johnathon and Kayden. Speaking of which," he looked around, "have you seen them?"

"Also packed up and headed out to Anura and Caladonia."

Robert still studied the bottom of his cup as if looking at it was going to fill it once again.

Jack stared at him in disbelief. Johnathon and Kayden had been his two closest friends growing up. "They left their farms? Their families have been here for—"

"Six and eight generations?" Robert nodded. "Yes, I know." He shook his head and let out a gusty breath. "Look, son. This famine . . . or whatever it is, is bad. The only work to be had around here is at that duke's property. And the only food around here are his beans."

"We've had droughts before."

"This is no drought. We have water, yes, but there is no food. The only way anyone has survived this long is through the food that's already been gathered and stored, and with us just at the beginning of summer, that's not much. If we'd known to prepare, we could have, but—" he broke off and simply shook his head.

As if seeing anew, Jack looked up and down the town's main street once more. The butcher and the baker had closed up shop, their windows and doors already boarded over. Josephine was in the process of boarding up her dressmaking building as well. The candlemaker's front looked empty, as did a number of family homes that lined the street. Dozens of people, many of whom were usually out tilling fields by this time of day, were wandering around as if in a daze. Then, as he turned to look up the north side of the street, a new question occurred to Jack.

"Did you ever meet Eva, Tamra's cousin, the one that moved in with her?"

Robert shook his head, but Jim nodded. "Blonde, tall, sweet." He paused. "A bit skittish?"

Jack nodded. "I was talking to her the night of the last dance, but she disappeared after that."

Robert, with his pipe in hand, puffed three gray smoke circles into the air that matched the exact shade of his beard. "She sure did. Word is that she was taken sometime that night or soon after. Her cousin denies it, though. Tamra just says she took off with some rich fellow." He puffed away silently for a moment before continuing. "The way she tells it, you'd think the girl had taken off with all her jewels and those babies of hers. Though the babies would be better off with the girl, if you ask me."

Jack felt as though someone had kicked him in the gut. She truly was gone. His mind immediately flew back to that night, trying to figure out when it must have happened. He had asked about her after she'd run off, but Tamra had insisted . . .

Tamra.

The duke.

"Whoa there." Jim nodded at Jack's hands. "Careful, or you're going to strangle that poor cow."

Jack immediately gave the rope some slack, but his anger didn't diminish. Someone needed to find her. Everyone should be looking. There hadn't been a case of a disappearing person in the area in years, and the last one he could remember was when old man Sutter had taken too much of a sleeping potion his wife had purchased out of town and had passed out in the loft of his barn. But, he realized as he looked around again, who would look for her? Those who were left were busy simply trying to survive.

If he had been on his own, he would've dropped the cow and everything else and run off in search of her himself, but he had his brothers to think about. If he had known things would be so bad, he would never have even brought them into town. Even now, as he kept an eye on them from just down the street, he couldn't help noticing more strangers eyeing his cow. None of them looked like they had much money, either, with which they planned to pay.

He looked back at his old friends. "Thanks for letting me know. Are you planning to leave, too?"

Jim and Robert looked at each other.

"I was raised on this land," Jim finally said slowly, the merriment gone from his eyes. "I plan to die here as well."

Robert shook his head and puffed another ring of smoke. "And when this fool passes out from hunger, I'll be along to drag his sorry self over the border to someplace with food." He paused. "But that won't be until we have no other choice." His voice softened. "As long as there's a choice, I'll stay."

Jack bid his friends goodbye, hoping it wasn't for the last time, and called for his brothers. As he did, a man passing by caught his eye. But instead of tipping his hat or smiling and looking away politely, the man watched their cow until they had turned the corner.

"You didn't sell the cow," Ray pointed out as he hopped down the road like a toad.

Jack pulled them close and told them in a low voice, "Stay close to me."

"Why?" Larry's brown eyes grew wide.

"The people here are desperate."

"Don't you trust our neighbors?" Ray looked around in alarm.

"Our neighbors I trust. But a lot of these folks I don't know."

"Papa always said we were supposed to help people in need."

"And if anyone wants a cup of water, I'll give it to them quicker than you can blink. But I won't have any stranger taking your food out from under my nose. As soon as we get home, I want you to grab your coats and good shoes and meet me at the barn. Tell Mother to do the same. We're taking the cow and horses and leaving."

"But what if Mother won't go?" Larry had turned a new shade of white.

Jack took a deep breath. "Then we're leaving without her."

All the way home, his mind was spinning. How had their happy little farming kingdom fallen so far while he was sick? It had only been three weeks. But now his hometown was filled with strangers as gaunt and desperate like he'd never seen. And it bothered him.

Guthward had always been known for its hospitality, and its people for their willingness to take strangers in and share in the abundance they worked so hard to grow. But now it seemed many of the people who would have helped one another were gone. And Jack didn't know where to turn.

And on top of all of that, Eva was missing.

Jack only let the boys leave his side when they were within a hundred yards of the house.

As they ran for the house, he planned. They would hitch up that old cart, the one too small to use for anything except the garden's produce. They would take the remaining oats and hay and anything else that they could find and put it in the cart. He would bring his father's old dagger, and the boys would take the few clothes they had. His mother, if she came at all, would insist on carrying the money, if they had any left.

But where would they go? Every relative he had was in Guthward.

"I hear you're trying to sell your cow."

Jack jumped. He whirled around just in time to see a scowling man in a long gray robe with . . .

He blinked. It had been a long time since his father had told him a bedtime story, but this creature looked like—

"Yes, I'm a fairy, if that's what you're wondering." The man rolled his eyes. "Now aren't you going to take my offer?"

"Your offer?" Jack tried to focus. This creature didn't look much like any of the fairies his father had told him stories about. From his wings, which looked too small to carry his tall frame, to the stubble that shadowed his face to his hair that looked as though he'd never seen a mirror, he was as unlike a fairy as anything Jack had ever imagined. Still, looks or no, if those stories had even an inkling of truth, his troubles might just be over.

Before he could utter a word about thriving crops or being whisked away to another kingdom, however, the fairy rolled up his sleeves. "Look, I'll make it worth your time."

The offer brought Jack somewhat back to his senses. "What do you need a cow for?" He looked the fairy up and down. "You've got magic. Can't you just make one appear out of thin air or something?"

"That's not how this works," the fairy snapped. "But if you'll trade the cow, I'll give you something better."

"Like what?"

The fairy dug into the pocket of his robe and pulled out a scrap of paper.

"Used parchment?" Jack was not impressed.

"No, no, no!" The fairy continued to dig through his pockets. There were more random bits and pieces of paper, twigs, several objects that sparkled, a blue speckled egg, and several pieces of fruit tucked into the flowing robe than Jack would have previously thought possible. "Ha!" Triumphantly, the fairy finally held up a fistful of something. "Now give me your hand."

But Jack backed up a step. "Not until you tell me what it is."

"Does it matter? You're getting something from a fairy. You should be groveling at my feet, begging to make the trade."

Jack gave a hard laugh. "I have two growing boys and a nagging mother to feed, and my crops have died without a clue as to why. And you're wondering why I'm not jumping for joy at the prospect of getting a surprise trade?"

With a huff, the fairy held out and opened his hand.

"Beans?" Jack stood up straight and ran his hand through his hair. "Five measly beans?"

"Magic beans!"

"Well, what do these magic beans do?"

The fairy flared his nostrils. "They'll take you to your true love."

Jack snorted. "If you knew anything about my love life, you would know it's nonexistent. And as if I have time to run off searching—"

"Look, do you want to find the girl or not?"

Jack had begun walking toward the barn again, but at these words he froze. He turned again. "Eva?"

The expression was so quick that Jack nearly missed it. But in the silent nod the fairy gave him, Jack recognized the emotion that flickered across the fairy's face for what it was.

"Wait, you know something, don't you?" He stepped back and studied the fairy again. But the fairy wouldn't meet his gaze. "That's it!" Jack cried. "You're guilty, aren't you?"

"I am not!"

"You've done something, and now you need someone else to fix your mess!" Jack rubbed his face. The weeks of being ill had caught up with him hours ago, and he felt more like fainting than taking on a quest. But if he could last a little longer, maybe he could use this to his advantage. And perhaps get a loaf of bread to boot. "Very well, if you want me to take your beans, then I first need some guarantees from you."

"What is it with you ungrateful humans and striking deals?" The fairy shook his head. "You're as bad as the woodcutter's little wicked one."

Jack hadn't the slightest idea as to what that meant, but he was too caught up in his plan to care.

"If I do this, I need you to provide food for my family until I bring the girl safely home."

The fairy gave an exaggerated eye roll. "Fine. Whatever. Anything else, your highness?"

Jack nearly laughed at the absurdity of the situation. He had a fairy on a string, and he was nearly ready to pass out from hunger. He'd better make the rest of the deal quickly. "Make the crops grow again."

"Can't. Next?"

"What?" Jack cried, but the fairy shook his unbrushed head.

"Other magic at work. Now what more do you want before I find someone else?"

Jack paused and thought. His family would be fed. Now he just needed them to be safe. "Give them a guard then, someone to keep away intruders while I'm gone."

"Very well. Rabid cat it is."

"Wha—"

"Now give me the cow and get a move on."

"Wait, why do you still need the cow?"

"These are magic beans, in case you forgot. I can't give them away for nothing!" And with that, the cow and the fairy were gone. And in Jack's hand lay five shiny green beans.

4

THAT'S WHY I CALLED YOU JACK

*J*ack cringed as another plate hit against the wall behind him, falling to the floor in a thousand pieces.

"I don't know what you're so upset about," he tried again. His answer was another flying plate.

"You're as dim as your father was!" His mother's face nearly matched the color of her graying copper locks. "How could you *give* him our cow?"

"For the last time, I didn't give it to him!" Jack fixed his mother with a glare. "He *took* it. But again, *you* were the one who wanted me to sell her, and since I made the deal, you and the boys will have food and protection until I finish this task. We'll be better off than anyone else nearby."

"No," his mother scowled so hard her thin shoulders shook, "*we* will be better off than them. *You* will have to find your own food!" She stomped out of the little kitchen and stuck her head out the door. "Larry! Ray! Get over here and bring a bag of oats while you're at it!"

"What about Jack?" Ray piped.

"He's finding his own supper tonight."

"Mother, really."

She whirled around to face him. "Let me see them then. Let me see these magic beans."

Jack rolled his eyes but reached into his pocket and pulled them out. Before he even finished opening his hand, however, she snatched them up and threw them out the window.

"Why would you do that?" Jack ran to the window and looked out, but it was no use. The beans had landed in the pigpen and were nowhere to be seen, already buried in the mud. He turned to his mother. "Why would you do that?"

"You'll learn one of these days not to go making decisions without me." She pointed to herself. "I own the deed! This is *my* farm, and that was *my* cow! I could have the constable arrest you for theft!"

"I'm trying to keep us alive! All you care about is . . . well, I don't know what you care about, but it certainly isn't your sons!"

"There you go again, making it all about you! I'll let you know that before you came along, I was my own person! I was beautiful and desired and—"

"Then you married Father! Yes, I know! But that was your decision! Then he died and—"

"And left me alone with this stinking farm and three boys. What do you expect of me?"

"To do your best!" Jack took a deep breath and ran his hand down his face. Fighting with his mother never did any good. "Look, I know I was never your favorite."

"You've got that right at least." She crossed her arms and refused to look at him, glaring out the window instead.

"But what I can't understand is why you're taking it out on the younger boys as well!"

"I take perfectly good care of your brothers."

"You tried to trade the farm for a carriage!" Jack cried in frustration.

"Well, I own the blasted place, don't I?"

Jack threw his hands in the air. "Where did you think we were going to live?"

She whirled around to face him. "It's not like you could do any better."

"You've never given me a chance!"

"Oh, poppycock. You quit every time things get hard. Just like your father. That's why I called you Jack."

Jack ignored her, but she went on.

"Remember the time you begged for a puppy? Wasn't a week before you said he was too hard to take care of, and I had to send him back."

"Mother, I was six."

But now she was smiling, a sure sign that, in her mind at least, she'd already won. "And then there was that riding competition you wanted to win. You practiced every day for three months, but when you showed up and saw the size of your competitors, you pulled out."

"I would have been the youngest by four years," Jack protested, but she went on, tying on her apron with that flat-lipped smile that drove him crazy.

"You know what, just forget it." Jack grabbed his hat and mashed it down on his head. He headed for the door but stopped on the threshold. "Just so you know, without those beans, I'll never finish my task, and the fairy will be angry!" He fixed her with a glare. "And he might come after you." He had the satisfaction of seeing her face pale slightly and her hands briefly pause before he slammed the door shut behind him.

"Doesn't change a thing about you!" she called through the window. "You're just like your father! He gave up on life, and you're no different!"

Jack ignored her as he went to the pigpen and leaned against the posts. Just when he'd thought he had everything figured out, his mother had intervened. Again. And now he had to figure out what to do before the fairy learned he'd lost the beans.

Before he could ruminate for too long, however, strange squelching sounds caught his attention. He peered closer at the mud.

Nothing.

With a snort of disgust, Jack was about to turn away, when five green vines shot out of the mud. Flying up into the sky, they continued to thicken and grow until they'd reached a height more than five times his house. Jack watched in awe as they then leaned in and wrapped themselves around one another, forming one giant braid of green vine.

His awe turned to panic, however, when the massive braid began to tilt. At first it was slow, but the more it leaned to the side, the faster it went until the entire piece finally fell and landed on the ground with a crash so great it shook the house behind him. Jack was knocked onto his back, and pain shot through his muscles and joints, which were still sore from his illness.

For a moment, he couldn't see what had become of the vine because he was too dizzy to get up. The headache that had plagued him during most of his convalescence returned, and he was rather sure his skin was on fire as well. Maybe, he thought to himself, the fairy wouldn't find him until he was dead, though whether starvation or his illness would end him first, he wasn't sure. Then his mother could decide what to do with the rabid cat.

Jack woke up sometime after dark, though he couldn't tell what hour it was or how long he'd been unconscious. Though he was within sight of the kitchen window, it appeared that his mother either hadn't noticed him or hadn't deigned to come out and at least cover him with a blanket. Not that that surprised him.

With a groan, he dragged himself to his feet and looked down at his body. He would have some nice bruises from the fall, but nothing looked or felt permanently damaged, and his fever seemed to have gone down again. But what was he going to do about the vine? And dinner?

Jack turned and gasped. The vine had not only wound itself tightly into a braid, but it had flattened itself into a perfectly smooth . . .

Was that a path?

Jack approached it carefully before leaning down and examining the vine more closely. In the light of the nearly full moon, he could make out its waxy green fibers. Putting one foot tentatively upon it, he prepared himself to leap back. But when nothing happened, he put his other foot on as well until he was standing on it with his full weight. The vine itself was firm but comfortable, much smoother than any dirt walking path he'd ever seen, or even the cobblestone streets like those in Sulta.

But where did it lead? He strained his eyes until they hurt, trying to make out the direction of the winding path in the darkness. From what he could see, it led west toward the low, ridged mountains.

Part of him, the boyish part that was far too much like his mother for his taste, always dreaming of something new, longed to follow the path. He'd never been farther from his home than two towns to the south, and he'd always longed to see the mountains. And if he went now, he would also get to rescue Eva, just as he'd agreed. That had been the deal after all.

The other part of him, however, hated to leave his brothers. Though his mother had never seemed to dislike them as much as she did him, he wasn't entirely sure she wouldn't sell the food once she figured out that it actually existed, and try to get herself a coach ride to anywhere but Guthward. And he could only be half sure that she would remember to take the boys.

He stood there, frozen on the strange vine path, for a long time. But as he tarried, a sound of footsteps caught his attention.

"Jack?" Ray called softly.

"Over here," Jack called, trying not to let his brother see just how weak he felt. "What are you doing up so late?"

"I came to bring you this." Ray held up an oatcake. It smelled of honey and dried dates. "Mother said not to give you any, but since you were sick . . ." Then he looked around. "Are you leaving us?"

Jack sighed. "I thought I had found a way to get us out of here." He looked longingly at the beanstalk road. "But I don't want to leave you . . ."

"Would you leaving mean we'd get food again?"

Jack nodded. "If the fairy was telling the truth, you should have protection as well."

Ray was silent for a long time. The sounds of bugs that were usually present were strangely missing, probably because of the lack of food. Finally, Ray looked back at his brother, his young face solemn.

"I think you should go." Then he cracked a small smile. "I'll handle Mother."

Jack pulled his brother into a tight hug before heading for the barn, new vigor in his steps. The oatcake filled his belly, and a rebel determination roared in his heart. He mounted a horse and pointed him toward the beanstalk road.

5

YOU NEED A WHAT?

*J*ack peeked through the leaves at the manor before him. He'd not seen a house so grand in his entire life. The wealthiest people in his town had two levels to their houses, and usually the lower level was a shop of some sort.

This house had five.

The journey to the beanstalk's end had taken him the entire night and a good part of the next morning. It probably would have been faster had he not been fighting the remnants of his illness and the continual stabs of hunger in his belly, as the oatcake hadn't even sustained him for a full hour. Thankfully, his horse, which he'd managed to sneak out of the barn, had eaten enough of the leftover hay to make the journey without collapsing, as Jack had worried he would.

The initial part of the walk was uneventful. The beanstalk wasn't on the road, but it followed along in the brush right next to it. His neighbors' fields looked just as dead as his. Their poor beasts pawed at the ground, picking at whatever remnants of plants they could find. But everything was dead. Corn stalks, beans stalks, alfalfa and hay fields, melon patches, rye, cotton, pecan trees . . .

even the weeds were dead, blackened and limp as a rags. Rolling plain after rolling plain of dead rot. The smell was enough to turn his stomach.

But after about eight hours, all that changed. It was difficult to see the transition at first, as the sun hadn't yet risen, but after a while, he was sure he saw a bit of green in the light of the moon. Surely his eyes were tricking him. It must be a symptom of his hunger or lingering illness. After another hour, however, when his horse stopped to eat an apple that had fallen on the flattened beanstalk, Jack admitted that perhaps his eyes weren't deceiving him after all. The trees and fields around him had really come to life! With this realization, he stopped his horse and gathered as many apples as his arms could hold before climbing back on to continue his journey, feeling more satisfied than he'd been in a long time.

After he'd gone on for long enough to give himself a stomachache from too many apples, but not long enough to see the rising of the sun, he spotted a light in the distance. At first he was sure it must be someone's campfire, someone trying to flee the kingdom no doubt. But the closer he got, the more he could see there were clearly more than one light.

By the time he came near enough to see the manor for what it was, the sun was just moments from rising, and it dawned on him that he was completely exposed. The vine had wound through groups of trees and down to the bottom of hills, and between those, the dark had been enough to hide him. But not far from the house stood a clump of trees that surrounded a little pool of water. Jack quickly moved his horse beneath their shelter just in time to hear the most enchanting sound.

Music, eerie and beautiful, rolled over the fields, which, he discovered in the growing light, were filled with soybeans. The melody cascaded up and down and high and low and back around again as though it were dancing through the stalks themselves.

As the song continued and the light grew stronger, Jack couldn't believe his eyes. Not only were the millions of stalks still alive, but they were the healthiest plants he'd ever seen, even compared to those on his own farm before the strange famine.

And they were swaying to the music.

Jack nearly fell over. He was halfway back on his horse and ready to send him flying to home, when the music stopped. Jack peeked through the branches again just in time to catch a movement. He lowered himself to the ground and crawled to the edge of the thicket where he would be less likely to be spotted. Then he waited for the movement again.

There, on one of the balconies, stood Eva. He hadn't noticed her before, but now that the light was better, he could see her standing behind something large. It looked like a harp, but without the full light of the sun, he couldn't be sure. He only managed to glimpse her, however, before she swished her skirts and moved back inside.

So the fairy had been right, and the beans had led him to Eva. Now he just had to get inside the manor, find the girl, and get out again. Then they would follow the beanstalk home, provided no one else noticed the giant green plant path that moved straight through private property and fields and even a few main roads.

Easy.

Jack tied his horse to a tree branch inside the thicket where he could reach apples from the branches and water from the pool, in case it took Jack a while to return. Then, staying in the shadows as much as possible, he darted across the immaculate front lot, trod lightly around the planted flowerbeds, avoided the little pools of floating lilies completely, and finally made it to the west corner of the big house. The sun broke over the horizon just as he threw himself into the house's shadow, and he gave a sigh of relief when he was finally no longer out in the open.

Around him he could hear the sounds of life beginning to stir. Men of all ages and sizes moved into the soybean fields, and through an open window in the house, he could hear people beginning to greet one another and discuss the day's chores. He crept along the wall to peer around to the back of the house, where he spotted not one barn, but three great storehouses out of which men and boys were already moving as they led oxen, donkeys, and horses, carried harvesting materials, and hauled empty sacks over their shoulders.

Jack snuck back to the window. Looking around, he pulled himself up and through. His balance, however, had been affected by his illness. His left arm gave way, and he crashed to the ground, just barely avoiding smacking the stone floor with his head. When he had finally righted himself, grateful no servants had walked by to witness his clumsiness, he slipped into the first open closet he spotted, where he could sit and plan the rescue.

Eva had been on the fifth floor. That meant he would need to find stairs. Peeking out from his hiding place, he spotted a staircase wide enough to fit four horses on it, side by side. The way it spiraled up into a huge hole in the ceiling reminded him of a snake making its way up a tree for an unsuspecting meal. He shuddered. Before he could imagine any other horrible comparisons for this strange big house, a scent caught his attention.

Well, it was more of a bundle of scents, really. After eating nothing but dry oats the day before, and far too many apples that morning, Jack's stomach gurgled loudly. It wasn't hard to spot the table just behind the staircase in what looked to be a dining room of sorts. The table was piled high with all the foods he had ever eaten and more.

Surely it wouldn't be too wrong to sneak a few bites before he continued his rescue. He would need his strength if he was going to return home again with a girl in tow.

He waited until a bell had rung and the servants cleared the room, then he dashed over to the table and began stuffing as many of the pastries, meat pies, sweet bread rolls, and little fruit pies into his pockets as he could.

"Jack?"

Jack turned slowly at the sound of the woman's voice. To his great relief, it was Eva.

Well, Eva, but draped in the most expensive materials and jewels Jack had ever seen. Her green gown shimmered in the light from a nearby window, and her golden hair was piled on top of her head and pinned there with dozens of shining green gems. It was a far cry from the simple country dress he'd last seen her wearing. While the color of the gown was somewhere between that of a bean pod and pond algae, it made her tall, slender figure look like she'd jumped right out of one of the fairy stories Jack's father had told him as a child.

Though Jack considered himself a gentleman, it wasn't without some effort that he was able to pull his eyes back up to her face and respond to her without sounding like a complete idiot.

"I . . ." Why was he here again? So much for not sounding like an idiot.

"You can't be here!" She hurried down the winding staircase and grabbed his arm before dragging him toward the door. She was surprisingly strong. "If the duke finds you, you could get hurt."

Before they reached the door, however, he was able to recover his senses. "I'm not here to run away!" He reached out and took her hand. The gesture felt strangely comfortable. "I came to rescue you!"

At first she seemed at a loss for words and looked almost like she might cry. But before Jack could soak up the unfamiliar feeling of pride in doing something right, she briefly closed her eyes and let out a sigh. "That's . . . very kind of you, but you need to go. Now. I don't want your family entangled in this mess, too." She frowned and pursed her lips for a moment before her eyes lit up. "Get out of Guthward and go to Astoria! My family lives in the capital. Take your family and find the wealthy woodcutters. Tell them where I am. Maybe they can contact the fairies—"

"Wait!" He stopped her. "The fairies already know!"

"They do?"

"Yes! One gave me the five beans that led me here."

Instead of seeming relieved, as he'd expected her to, she stiffened. "Was this a . . . male fairy?"

He nodded. "Tall and thin with a scraggly beard, tiny girlie wings. And quite grumpy."

"Oh no." Eva put her hands on her face.

"What's wrong?"

"That was my fairy godfather, Mortimer." She shook her head and threw up her arms helplessly. "I might as well start naming the children now. Duke One, Two, and Three."

"Hold on," he said, taking her by the shoulders. "What's so wrong with the fairy? I mean, his beans *did* lead me straight to you."

"Mortimer is a terrible godfather. He's more interested in experimenting with his magic than he is in any of our *mundane* human lives, something he's quite keen on reminding my family any time he's near."

"He seemed pretty interested in getting you home."

"Because it's *his* fault I'm here in the first place!"

Before he could respond, another voice sounded in the hall, and Eva paled. "Oh no," she muttered. Footsteps and more voices became audible. She whirled around. "Just play along!"

"What?"

"Just do what I say!"

The duke walked in just as Eva faced the entryway once again. The little man was somehow even less impressive than he had been during their first meeting. Despite his age, the man's pate was already beginning to shine in the direct light, and the waistcoat he wore was far too tight for the paunch that strained its buttons. He was sweating profusely, though his clothes looked too neat for him to have been laboring outside with the other men, but sweat ran down his face as though he'd been working in the fields for hours.

"Eva," he said with his odd little smile as he walked in, trailed by four servants.

"You're up early," she said in a tight voice.

The duke stopped and stared at Jack. "Who is this?"

Jack opened his mouth to answer, but Eva cut him off.

"He came here on business."

The duke frowned. "What could he—"

"And I want to hire him!"

Everyone, including Jack, looked at her as though she'd lost her mind, but she kept her back and shoulders straight and her eyes on the duke. But what was she talking about? Jack certainly had no desire to be employed in the duke's services.

"What for?" the duke finally asked.

"I need him as my cupbearer!"

"You need a what?"

Jack nearly echoed the duke. What was she getting him into?

But Eva didn't so much as bat an eye. "My cupbearer," she said just as firmly, putting her hands on her hips. Then she rolled her eyes dramatically and huffed, as though they were all uncommonly stupid. "A cupbearer," she repeated, "is someone who will follow me around with a goblet of cider or tea or wine or something at all times I am awake." She nodded, as though this were the most logical request in the world. "Then I'll never be thirsty again." She fixed her steady gaze on the duke. "And you won't have to continue running off to fetch a drink for me on our walks."

Jack thought this was about the most bizarre situation he'd ever witnessed, much less been a part of, but the duke's eyes lit up.

"That is a splendid idea, my harp! You shall have your cupbearer, and I shall have a chance to read you my poetry uninterrupted." He turned to a manservant just behind him. "Get this fellow a uniform, tray, and several goblets." He turned back to Eva. "You shall have your drinks, I shall read you my poetry uninterrupted, and everyone will be happy. Now, I must go to my library and organize some new ledgers, but I look forward to tonight with great anticipation." He turned to Jack then and opened his mouth. Instead of speaking, however, he merely paused for a moment and tilted his head thoughtfully. Jack hoped desperately that he had forgotten their meeting at the party several weeks before, and for one long minute was sure he would be found out. But eventually, the duke only said, "Hm," before turning and climbing the stairs.

6

I REALLY AM SORRY

"My name," the manservant said, turning to Jack after the duke was gone, "is Cumberfold, and I am the steward of these grounds. Follow me." His words were polite enough, but the tone of his voice made his opinion of Jack quite clear, his whiskers twitching with each word he spoke. Not that Jack cared. He would be gone, hopefully, before he had time to wear the ridiculous uniform. But before he could follow the man anywhere, Eva stood in their path.

"This man is not going anywhere until he's had a bath."

Both Jack and his long-whiskered guide stared at her blankly. Jack wanted desperately to ask her what she was up to. She wasn't making her rescue very easy. But no matter how hard he pleaded with his eyes, she ignored him and kept her razor-sharp gaze on the manservant.

"I beg your pardon, milady?"

"I said, he needs a bath before he puts on that uniform." When the man still didn't move, she crossed her arms with a scoff. "If you can't smell him, you must have broken your nose. The fellow's been on the road, and I want him clean before he starts following me around."

Cumberfold finally shook his head and gave a little sigh before turning to a younger manservant nearby. "Grab Hotches and you two draw a bath for . . ." He turned to Jack. "What's your name?"

"People call me Jack."

Cumberfold frowned a little, but he continued. "Draw a bath for Jack. Put it in the . . ." He stopped and pursed his lips for a moment. "The smallest guest room in the north wing. Give him his uniform there and bring him to the kitchen when he's done. Marcel can explain his duties."

Jack considered making a smart comment about the complex difficulties being a cupbearer must involve, but a sharp look from Eva convinced him otherwise.

He followed the young servant down several large hallways, each containing more rooms than the last. The floor they walked on was made of polished wood, so shiny Jack felt a little guilty about the mud he knew he was tracking in on his boots. Something for someone else to clean. From the look on his guide's face, Jack guessed he was thinking the same thing as well.

It wasn't long before Jack had been left alone in a room with a tub of water. Before the footsteps had faded behind the door, however, they came running back. He opened the door just in time to see a boy, not much older than Larry, holding out a little green cube of soap.

"Miss Eva says you're to use this," the boy said before turning and dashing away.

Jack shook his head as he looked down at the object he'd been given. After a sniff, it was clear that this was not just any soap, but one that smelled strongly of . . . something sweet that Jack couldn't name. In fact, it had a rather feminine smell to it. The more he got to know Eva, the stranger she was becoming. Still, he had made a bargain with the fairy, and odd or not, she didn't deserve to be stuck anywhere close to the duke. So he turned back to the tub with a sigh. He would simply have to play along until they found their chance for escape. And escape they would.

He studied the round wooden tub before getting in. Jack had always bathed in a river not far from his house. He'd heard of such privileges before, but never had he actually experienced a hot bath. One foot in the icy tub, however, made it very clear that he was not about to get a hot bath here either. He finished washing as quickly as he could, trying to use the soap as little as possible, and then threw on the confining clothes he'd been left by the servant—green trousers that were so dark they were nearly black, with a white undershirt and a green vest on top.

Jack had never felt more like a plant.

Before leaving the room, he took a deep breath and tried to ready himself. Whatever lay on the other side of the door was sure to be strange if this morning had been any indication.

Upon opening the door, however, instead of a servant's face, Jack found himself staring into a pair of soft brown eyes. She motioned for silence and then handed him a round silver platter and a goblet, and beckoned for him to follow.

Jack hadn't known any building could be so big. He'd heard of the manors and castles in the capital, but as he'd never visited Tulkarnie himself, he'd only been able to conjure up small pictures in his head of what such bastions must look like. But here, as they darted in and out of shadowed halls, he found himself more and more in awe of the dozens and dozens of rooms one building could hold.

After about ten minutes of sneaking through the house, they finally came to a room that was made up nearly entirely of windows. Plants of every shape and size filled aisle after aisle, and the corners were too full of ivy to even bother visiting. The ceiling reached up nearly three stories high, and the room itself was almost large enough to fit Jack's cottage inside twice over.

"My friends would never—" Jack began.

"Shhh!" Eva put a finger up to her lips before running back to the entrance. Only when the doors were shut behind them did she let out a loud sigh. She looked up at him. "You have no idea how hard it is to live here. It is exhausting to be that demanding."

He let out a little laugh. "You caught me off guard, I'll admit. I hadn't planned on coming here for any sort of work."

She took the tray from him and fingered its filigreed edges carefully. "I apologize for that. It's just . . . that's the only way I've been able to get anything at all done since arriving." She put her hands to her temples and rubbed them. "Soon after I arrived, I had a rather unladylike outburst in front of the duke. I didn't mean to, but his incessant talk and constant presence had been wearing on me. One of the servants asked me something, and I began to shout." A near smile played on her lips. "The duke was shocked, and it was then that I realized behaving like a petulant child was the only way to get what I wanted around here, at least as long as he thinks he has a chance of wooing me and thus tries to fulfill my ridiculous wishes." She shook her head incredulously. "So, unfortunately, I have continued to be petulant and childish just so the duke knows he can't run my life. At least not completely." She let out a deep sigh.

"I'm sorry to interrupt your thoughts, but," he glanced to his left at the balcony set out through the wall of windows, "shouldn't we be escaping now that we're alone? I did come to rescue you after all."

"Wait." She held her hand up and ran over to the window wall. After a moment, she beckoned him. "It's clear. Come see. Just stay back here, out of sight."

He followed her to the balcony and then stood where she indicated, about ten feet back. Even from his hidden position, he could see that the green-room balcony looked down over fields and fields of what appeared to be bean plants.

"There," she said. "Look down at the closest field to the left. See those men? The duke is the short one in the middle."

As she said his name, the duke looked up at the balcony and waved frenetically. She didn't return the gesture, just stared down with a look of contempt.

"I'm under watch at all times."

Jack looked around. "I don't see any guards." Still, he pitched his voice low.

"It's not human guards I'm concerned with. The duke has little spells tied all around the property. If I move past one, it will be cast, and something awful will happen." She shivered. "I tried escaping three times that first week."

"What happened?"

"The first time, one of my feet turned to lead. It returned to normal the next day, just in time for my second escape, when I lost my vision for another whole night."

"What happened the third time?"

She shuddered. "You don't want to know. My point is that the duke may appear to be a dimwit, and generally, he is. But he's conniving and just clever enough to know how to use magic here despite the land's natural propensity against it. My magic, at least." She tilted her head and studied Jack, the gold in her brown eyes glinting in the sun's rays. "That's why I sent you the soap. You have magic on you. Or you did, at least." Her forehead puckered. "The magic felt too close to mine, and the duke will be suspicious if he isn't already. He keeps some fairy trinket on him that changes colors when magic is near."

Jack stared at her, his mouth falling open. This certainly wasn't going to be as easy as he thought.

"I thought he was trying to woo you."

"Oh, he is. He's just too infatuated with himself to realize that one doesn't kidnap a woman and place spells on her in order to win her heart."

"Then how do we—" Before he could say anything else, however, his knees buckled, and he was only saved from slamming his head against a workbench by Eva, who caught him and pulled him to a nearby empty seat. He expected her to drop him there and step back, but she instead pressed her hand to his forehead.

"What are you doing?" he asked. Not that her cool hand didn't feel nice pressed up against his forehead. He actually would have liked for it to stay there.

"You're burning up!" She put both of her hands on his face.

Jack didn't so much as blink. Never before had any woman, including his mother, touched him so gently.

"Stay here." Her words were commanding, and he didn't dare disobey. She got up and went to the door and peeked out. "Taylor," she called after a moment. "Get Mrs. McConnell. Have her bring me a bowl of soup, buttered toast, and a kettle of tea." A reply was made, and Eva scowled. "Does it matter if I'm hungry again? I don't care what the duke says! Get the housekeeper!"

When the door was closed again, Jack felt a sudden wave of dizziness and was forced to lie down on the bench.

"Well," she said, "I suppose it's a good thing that we're not going anywhere tonight. You wouldn't make it very far if we did."

But he shook his head and tried to push himself into a sitting position. "We have to go. I made a deal."

"You're not going anywhere in this condition. You, Jack, are very sick."

"What, are you my mother?" He tried to laugh, but it really wasn't that funny, considering she'd given him more attention in the fifteen minutes they'd been together then his mother had since . . . well, since he could remember. "Besides," he said, "didn't you say you have some sort of magic, yourself? Could we use that to escape?"

"I doubt it. My magic is . . . different." She shivered and wrapped her arms around herself. "But even if I could, I wouldn't. At least, not yet."

"What?" Jack was hallucinating. He had to be. For he was rather sure that the young woman who had been abducted by possibly the most ridiculous figure on the continent had just said that she wouldn't use her magic to escape.

She lowered her voice and glanced at the door. "The duke is up to something. I don't know what he's planning, but whatever it is, it's not good. Not for me or for you or for the kingdom."

A knock on the door interrupted them.

"Are you feeling well, Miss Eva?" A skinny woman, probably a good ten years his mother's senior, peeked in. In her hands, she balanced a tray with a big bowl, several plates, and several goblets and cups.

"I am, Mrs. McConnell," Eva replied, "but I'm afraid my cupbearer isn't in the best of health since he arrived this morning."

The older woman gave Eva a wan smile. "My lips are tied shut, Miss Eva."

Eva took the tray. "Which is why I called you. Thank you so much!"

As soon as the door was shut, Eva set the tray down and expertly began to move its contents around, rummaging until she evidently found what she wanted.

"Who's that?" Jack asked.

"The head housekeeper. Unlike her master, she's quite kind."

"Do you think she would help us escape?"

"No." Eva sighed as she stirred the tea. "She's kind, but the staff here is terrified of that man." Then, with a nod to herself, she picked up a spoon and blew on a bite of soup before bringing it to his mouth.

Without thinking, he automatically opened his mouth, and a big spoonful of the most flavorful soup was shoved inside. "What are you doing?" he asked after automatically swallowing.

"You're sick. And I'm taking care of you. What else would I be doing?" She gave a little laugh. "I don't know what you do for sick people in your house, but in mine, we try to keep them from dying."

Awe and shame warred inside Jack. His mother had never put as much care into one of her sick sons as Eva had in the simple brush of her hand against his forehead. Instead of admitting this, however, he changed the topic.

"It doesn't matter." He shook his head, a mistake, as it set the world spinning. "We have to go. I told your godfather I'd bring you home."

"I . . . I think I want to stay."

"Wait, you're telling me you want to stay here with this duke—"

"No. I mean we need to figure out his plans and then stop him!"

"Whoa, now!" Jack rubbed his eyes. "I didn't agree to make enemies with some crazy duke with a magic obsession. I agreed to bring you home. Nothing more. Life is bad enough as it is without this complicated mess. All I want to do is get you to safety and take my family as far from Guthward as our horses can carry us."

"What do you mean *bad enough*?" She frowned as she stirred the tea.

"I mean that every single plant in the kingdom has died except for what you have here on this farm. The only thing anyone has to eat is beans, and now that I know the kingdom's only food source is coming from the slightly insane second heir to the throne, I want to stay here even less." Jack sat back, breathing heavily. Before he could try to catch his breath, however, he felt cool fingers beneath his chin. They guided his mouth to the cup of tea she had prepared and was now holding up to his lips.

As he drank, Jack tried to wrap his mind around how crazy this girl was turning out to be. But as upset as he wanted to be with her, anger was difficult when she was doing her best to nurse him back to health.

"Don't you see?" she asked.

Jack made the mistake of meeting her big brown eyes.

"If we don't stop him now, who will?" Her pleas were gentle, like a spring rain against the roof. "He's using my magic to control the entire kingdom's food supply. If we don't—"

"Wait," Jack said, "he's using *your* magic? *You* are the one doing this?" He gestured out beyond the balcony at the green fields below.

Eva nodded solemnly.

"Why don't you just tell him no? Or better yet, why don't you use your magic against him?"

Eva's eyes widened and she shook her head emphatically. "First of all, he says he'll hurt my family if I leave. And even worse," she shuddered, "as if that were possible, he says he'll kill the king."

Jack studied her, not sure if she could really be telling the truth. Surely the duke wasn't that powerful.

As if reading his thoughts, she nodded. "I tried to stop once. About three days after I was taken. But when I told him I was done, he said that he has someone in the king's personal circle. All they're waiting for is a word from him."

"Well," Jack said slowly, "then I'll go warn the king." He wasn't sure how a dirty farmer would gain an audience with the king, but a warning about a plot against the king's life would probably do the trick.

"I've already tried that. I sent two young men I paid off in jewels.

"And?"

"Nothing. I never heard from them again, and the duke tells me almost daily that his men are still there." She sighed. "Besides," she visibly shuddered, "I don't even want my magic. Nothing good comes from this kind of power. I don't know how to use it. I don't even know what I'm doing when I use it as he says. I'm not going to risk the people here or anyone else by trying to use something I shouldn't even own. It's too dangerous." She broke a biscuit and buttered it before holding it out to him, but Jack ignored it.

"So you wouldn't escape, even if we found a way to warn your family? You wouldn't use your magic even for something as simple as escape?"

She slowly shook her head. "I can't let him kill the king. Or anyone else. I have to stop him myself."

Jack stared at her for a long time. His thoughts warred within him. On one hand, it was impossible not to be impressed by her kindness and her bravery. He hadn't been attended to with that kind of care since his father had died. On the other hand, however, he had his brothers to think about. And if Eva refused to be rescued, the fairy was sure to end their provision and protection.

"Well," Jack rose unsteadily to his feet, "I'm sorry. I really did want to rescue you. But I can't stay here and gamble with the lives of my family."

"You're leaving?" She stared up at him, her lips parting as she accused him with her eyes. "You're just . . . quitting?"

Jack refused to meet her gaze as he turned and walked to the door. How his mother would crow with triumph if she could see him now.

Eva hurried after him, her skirts rustling as she threw herself between him and the door. "The duke never lets anyone outside at dusk or before dawn."

"That's well and good because I'm leaving now."

"But he'll see you! He knows all of his workers and has informants everywhere!"

"Fine. Then I'll leave when it starts to get dark, before twilight."

She shook her head. "If anyone catches you on his lands before dark and you're not indoors, he'll kill you! If you leave tonight, you'll never make it off his lands in time."

"Why not?"

"Because he doesn't want anyone to see my magic. Everyone here knows the crops have something to do with me, but he's keeping my real secret as quiet as possible, meaning he'll kill if he has to, to maintain silence. I've seen him do it." She looked him up and down briefly. "And you're in no condition to make it off his lands by dusk."

"I snuck around this morning without being detected, and I'll do it again." He reached around her for the door handle. But guilt made him meet her gaze for one long moment before he opened it. "I really am sorry," he whispered. Then he slipped out and made his way down the hall.

7

DON'T CALL ME THAT

*E*va slumped in her seat during supper. What had begun as a bright and glorious day full of promise and hope had spiraled out of the sky and crashed to the ground, like the flying candle Martin had once tried to invent and released out of his second-story window. Just like her mother's favorite plate Martin had used to build the contraption, Eva's world was now in pieces, and she was even more discouraged than before.

"No," the duke said as he walked in, surrounded by his usual entourage, "I want the paint in that room to be white with touches of green. It helps me think."

"Very well," Cumberfold said, tucking a ledger under his arm and pulling another out of his jacket. "What about the Golden Goose project?"

"We'll discuss that later." The duke had turned his sharp little eyes on Eva and grinned a little too widely. "Good evening, my harp. I hope you're well. Did you enjoy your time in the green room?"

"As much as ever." Eva focused intently on her plate. "And don't call me that." How she wished Rynn were with her. Rynn would have set the awful duke straight long ago. But Eva's tongue wasn't as sharp as her sister's, nor would it do any good to go tearing up in front of the duke.

"I got a new bauble today!" His round face lit up as he pulled a little ball from his pocket. "Do you want to see?"

Eva eyed the ball suspiciously. "What does it do?"

"It's the most wonderful thing! You throw it, and it temporarily paralyzes the first thing it hits." He took aim at poor Cumberfold.

"No, thank you," Eva said quickly, meeting eyes briefly with a seemingly relieved Cumberfold.

"Why not?"

Eva put her fork down and folded her hands, as though she were talking to a small child. "The last bauble you showed me was supposed to put out fires. It started one and nearly burned down the house. And the one before that hit Janis in the leg and put her out of work for a week while the physician attempted to remove the frogs that had become stuck to her legs. So no, for the sake of the staff, I am not interested in seeing any more of your *baubles*."

The duke looked somewhat deflated before sitting and eyeing his food. "I see you took your new . . . what did you call him? Cupbearer with you?" His voice was pleasant, almost singsong in its cadence.

Drat. She'd hoped to keep Jack hidden in the green room to avoid suspicion. But as ever, the duke was one step ahead. "He fell ill soon after we arrived. I wanted him to rest." That much was true, at least.

"You haven't eaten anything," the duke said, his mouth full of jellied meat. "Are you ill, too?"

How she wished she were. She gave him a sharp look instead. "Aside from being abducted and forced into marriage against my will?"

"You're going to be queen. When that happens, you can move your family to the palace and give them whatever they want. I don't see how that's anything but beneficial to you all."

"They've been down that road before," she muttered.

"What's that?"

"Nothing."

"It's rude to mumble, my harp. Very unqueenly."

There were many things Eva would like to do and say that would be very *unqueenly*. Like mash the duke's face in his jellied meat, for instance. Instead, however, she allowed silence to ensue, the only sounds the tapping of the servants' feet as they walked to refill plates and cups. And Eva was fine with that. She had a raging headache. Unfortunately, the duke could not allow the beautiful silence to continue too long uninterrupted.

"Where is the boy now?" As if the duke were very much older and wiser than Jack. He couldn't be older than twenty and seven or eight.

Eva kept her eyes on her food, aware of the way his sharp eyes were measuring her. "He traveled far to get here, and he's obviously not had enough to eat. He needs to rest if he's to accompany us on our walk tomorrow."

"Do you know him from somewhere before?" The duke casually sipped his wine. Eva tried not to gag when he smacked his lips after every swallow. "You seemed to be rather familiar with him. Or at least, his intentions."

"I only met him the same night you did." She finally looked up, attempting to appear as detached as possible. "The night you kidnapped me."

The duke watched her, unblinking, for a long moment. Then his eyes widened and he leaned back. "Ah, yes! The farm boy. I'd forgotten. I'm curious, though. Out of all the young men we have working my lands, why him? He's not that attractive, if I may say so."

Eva took a drink, swallowing the words about the duke's *attractiveness* that she desperately wanted to spew, and shrugged. "He comes from the same town as my cousin. I thought he might have news as to their welfare."

"That was thoughtful of you, of course, but I've told you that you shall know anything that might need knowing."

"Forgive me if I find it difficult to take you at your word." She stabbed a pile of spinach with her fork, not bothering to eat it with any of the sweet foods on the plate. It would taste bitter anyway, knowing that the rest of the kingdom was barely surviving on beans . . . and knowing that she was to blame. After a few attempts at chewing, however, she could hardly manage to swallow. She dropped her fork on the plate with a loud clank.

"What is all this for anyway?" She stared at him as hard as she could. It was easier to do when she pictured Sophie in his chair instead of the duke. "Why starve the kingdom in the first place?"

"I'm not starving them. They're getting beans, which I am generously sending out to all corners of the map."

"But why?" she asked in exasperation. "Why do you need me when you have a thousand magical baubles and trinkets just lying around?"

"All in good time, my dear."

"Any why beans?"

"Because I like beans. I'm actually being rather generous, you know. Wait. Where are you going?"

"I'm not hungry." Eva shoved her chair back in before a servant could do it for her.

"I look forward to our walk tomorrow!" the duke called after her as she hurried up the spiral staircase to her room. "Don't forget to wear comfortable walking slippers."

Eva didn't acknowledge him. Instead, she lifted the front of her skirt and ran. And she didn't stop until she'd thrown herself on her bed, where she lay weeping until her tears could come no more.

Eva's mood was no better the next morning when she awakened.

For as soon as her eyes opened, she was reminded of three awful truths.

She was responsible for killing the livelihoods of the kingdom that relied on farming for its main exports.

She was still expected to marry the duke.

Jack was gone.

She never awoke looking forward to the day. Not anymore. And a day full of the duke and his insufferable poetry just might push her past the point of sanity, particularly after the evening of tears that she'd attempted unsuccessfully to sleep off. But if she refused to walk with him, he'd show up wherever she was and read his poetry anyway. At least if they were outside in the shade of the apple trees, she could try to focus on the aspects of nature, and perhaps discover something new about his plans. For all the man's oddities, he was an excellent schemer, but there had to be a way to unravel his mystery and stop him.

One couldn't possibly be as clueless as the duke without some vulnerability.

Before she could dwell for too long on her dire situation, however, a little bell was rung outside her door.

"It's time, my harp," the duke called from the hall.

Eva sighed and rolled out of bed. She had long suspected that he was using her evening song for mischief, but until Jack had informed her, she hadn't thought her song capable of killing the entire kingdom's crops. But then how did the duke's survive?

As she walked toward the eastern balcony, she wondered suddenly if the placement of her songs had something to do with their abilities. At first, she'd simply believed the two harps to exist simply because of his obsessive organization. After all, the man couldn't stand for his food to touch on his plate, and he truly had ledgers of information on everything, including the servants' dusting schedule for the basement. It would only make sense for him to want his songs to come from different instruments. Or different directions.

"The sun is almost risen," he called again in that gratingly patient voice.

"I'm coming!" she snapped back as she seated herself at the instrument. And as her fingers began to pluck at the strings, she found herself wishing greatly to strangle him with the instrument pieces instead.

Though it was morning, and she couldn't have asked for a more beautiful sunrise, she struggled. Playing the song was growing harder by the day. What had once been one of her favorite melodies, sweet and gentle like the dance of many sunbeams, was quickly becoming hollow and haunting. She could play the right notes, of course, but her heart wasn't in it.

What would she do when all her joy was gone, and not even the duke's crops would grow? What would he do? What would the people of Guthward do?

"Good morning, Miss Eva."

Eva turned, her torturous song finally over, and gave the head housekeeper a tired smile. "Good morning, Mrs. McConnell."

Mrs. McConnell hurried over to the wardrobe, her slight limp giving her shoes uneven taps across the floor. "Having a down morning are we?"

Eva froze. "How did you know?"

"That song wasn't exactly cheery now." The housekeeper pulled out two green dresses and stared at them before tossing them both to the side and attacking the wardrobe again. "His lordship won't be pleased if his crops have another bad day." Her tone wasn't unkind or even cautionary. She was just stating the facts that Eva was painfully aware of.

"I'm doing my best."

"I know you are. There, what about this one?" She pulled a gown out and held it up.

Eva made a face.

"What about that cupbearer fellow you hired yesterday?" The housekeeper chuckled. "I should think he would give you something to be happy about." She laughed a little more loudly. "I might be older than the two of you, but that *face*. I can see why you would want him around all day."

Eva felt herself color. Staring at Jack's face all day hadn't been exactly what she'd had in mind when she'd tried to give him employment. Rather, she'd felt better at the thought of having another man constantly present when she and the duke were out and about. Not that Jack would have been able to stop the duke from making any advances, particularly with the duke's seemingly endless supply of little magic tricks he kept in his pockets. But still, having someone else who seemed at least halfway decent had been highly appealing at the time, as she'd tried desperately to come up with a way to keep him near.

Not that his face wasn't handsome. His sharp jawline and high cheekbones had caught her attention that first night at the dance, and the intensity of his slate-gray eyes, like a thunder cloud over the mountain, had made her look twice. His thick blond hair had been messy, but not in an unattractive way. After last night, however, she wasn't sure exactly how attractive she would ever find him again. Not after the way he'd simply . . . left.

Now, that's not fair, a voice in her head that sounded much like Rynn's chided. *He has a family to look after. You would hesitate, too, if the twins were counting on you.* Eva shook her head. She was still alone and the kingdom was still in danger, and she really had no desire to listen to reason this morning. Even if it did sound like Rynn.

Once she was dressed and ready, she shook her shoulders out and inhaled deeply before letting the air out slowly through her nose. Today wasn't just another walk with the duke, she told herself. It was another opportunity to thwart him. Yes, that was it. Now if only she could keep that attitude when her greatest desire became to smack her host because his poetic allusions went too close to improper for her taste.

When she exited her chambers, however, she was shocked to

find not only the duke's round face, beaming at her, but another young man standing behind him. And in his hand was a tray full of drinks.

Jack had returned.

Eva tried not to let her relief show on her face as she forced herself to meet the duke's eyes.

"Good morning, Eva." He held his arm out. "Ready? I have something new today!"

"Another poem?"

"No, actually. I've begun to get the feeling that you don't share my enthusiasm for poetry."

"Whatever gave you that idea?"

"So I tried something else."

Eva made a choking sound as she tried to swallow the hysterical laughter that threatened to bubble out. Jack quickly handed her a goblet, which she immediately downed and then regretted it. The mulled wine was always overspiced in the duke's kitchen, and now she would be tasting it for hours. Oh well. Perhaps the wine would boost her confidence.

The duke continued to watch her face intently as they walked, showing no sign of fear or annoyance at her outburst. "I've written a story. It's about our love and what it would be like if you were in a tower guarded by a dragon, and I were a grand knight who had come to rescue you."

Eva knew she shouldn't encourage him, but she couldn't help it. "You would rescue me? Why would you do that?"

They came to a stop at a door that led out to the back pastures where the natural apple groves grew. "No woman ought to suffer the contemptible situation of being locked away against her will." He looked at Jack. "Well?"

It took Jack a moment to understand what the duke expected, and Eva cringed as he tripped and nearly spilled the wine in his attempt at opening the heavy door with his one free hand. The duke passed through first. As Eva walked through as well, however, Jack leaned in.

"He does know he's the dragon, does he not?"

Eva shushed him but couldn't keep a straight face as she rejoined the duke. No, from the confident beam that he still wore, she doubted it very much.

At first Eva thought she might at least be amused by the change in his wooing tactics. But she was wrong. The prose was even worse.

" . . . as the sun beat down on the isolated gray tower, the fair maiden leaned out the window and sighed to herself as she imagined the knight taking her in his arms and kissing her with the passion of a million bees. His hairy, manly touch stung her skin, and his breath stank of onion, for that is what he'd had for dinner the night before, along with roast boar and a wineskin of ale he'd purchased in Dibonshire three weeks prior. It had been a lovely meal. But even the smell of his breath could not put her off, for she longed for his strong, royal hands to wrap themselves around her—"

"Ow!" Jack cried out.

The duke turned around and stared at him, pressing his lips tight in what Eva recognized as his look of disgust. "Do we need to send you to the physician?" His voice was thick with condescension.

"No." Jack spoke through his teeth, his eyes slipping Eva an accusing glance before returning to the ground.

Eva hid her smile. Her little kick had been well aimed, and Jack's shin would be bruised for a week. But that was nothing compared to what the duke would have done had he seen Jack's shoulders shaking with his quiet snickers the way Eva had.

"Where was I? Oh, yes. Before Joseph—"

"Jack."

"That's what I said. Now . . . Um, wait. Excuse me for a moment." He cleared his throat, but as he looked down at his paper, something caught his eyes. To Eva's great joy, he quickly folded the paper and shoved it in his coat pocket. Then he pulled a thin black ledger from his jacket and whipped out a quill pen, wetting it on his tongue before getting it to work.

The gesture itself wasn't unusual, as he was always writing this or that in a ledger, but this one was different. Because on the ledger's binding were the words *Golden Goose* scratched into the leather, barely legible from where she stood.

"What's that project?" she asked, for once not having to feign interest.

"Which one?"

"Golden Goose. Cumberfold said something about that last night at supper as well."

He stared at her for a long moment before blinking and pulling his story from his pocket again. "Nothing you need to worry your pretty little head about, my dear. Now, where was I? Ah, yes. She longed for his strong, royal hands to wrap themselves around her delicate waist. She wanted him to mash his bearded face against hers and kiss her as though . . ."

And on and on the story went. And as awful as it was, Eva found a kind of sinister glee in knowing that Jack had to suffer along with her. Served him right for leaving her last night. Eventually, though, enough workers came up to ask the duke questions that he took her hand in his clammy fingers, and Eva had to consciously keep herself from grimacing. It was like being clutched by a frog.

"I am sorry, my harp, but I beg your leave for the time being. I am going to visit the Countess of Sill Cotter, and I have a number of business needs that must be attended to."

A wild thought hit Eva, and without thinking, she grabbed his clammy hand again. "Mightn't I go with you this time? I mean," she did her best to look earnest, "if I'm to be queen one day, shouldn't I get to know your peerage as well?"

"Ah, finally thinking productively. I'm afraid not, though." He dropped her hand and turned to go back to the house. "You have work that must be done here. And," he paused at the edge of the apple grove, "I do expect your work to be done properly. And you, Jerry!" he aimed a stern look at Jack, "I expect your conduct to be beyond reproach. None of this business should be conducted alone. You may act as cupbearer as long as you're in public." He smiled sweetly at Eva. "I'll not have my future wife's reputation questioned."

Jack, shaking his head slowly, watched him until the duke had gone into one of the storehouses. "He's worried about your reputation . . . after writing *that*?" He rubbed his temples. "I'm not the scholar I wish I was, but even I can say that *that* was akin to dropping a hammer on my foot repeatedly."

But Eva wasn't smiling. Instead, she watched him carefully. He sobered quickly when he turned and saw her expression.

"Before we do anything else, I need to know two things," she said softly.

His gaze went to the ground. "Yes?"

"First of all, are you back to help me finish this? Or do you plan to run at the first sign of trouble?"

He nodded. "I'm sorry for yesterday. That was wrong of me. I said I would help you." His jaw tightened and his eyes sparked, though at what Eva couldn't tell. "And I'm going to."

Eva nodded slowly. "My second requirement is to know what your intentions are."

He looked at her as though she'd sprouted a third arm.

"I'm here to bring you home."

"I mean . . ." She could feel the blush rising to her face, but if she didn't say it now, she never would. "Will your . . . actions continue to be noble when we're alone together? Because if we're going to figure this out, we're going to be alone quite a bit."

At this, his eyes widened for a moment, and his cheeks reddened as well. "Oh. Of course. I mean, I would never do anything . . . untoward."

Eva finally let herself smile as she breathed a sigh of relief. "I thought so. I just needed to know for sure." She laughed a little, suddenly feeling close to giddy. "My brother would have my head if he knew what I was about to do alone with another man."

Jack didn't say anything, but glanced at her nervously.

She laughed again. "And if you're worried about me seducing you, you needn't fear. I couldn't charm a drunk. Or at least, my sister is always saying so."

He gave her a funny look, and she didn't miss his eyes sweeping up and down her form cautiously. For a moment, he looked as though he might make a reply. But instead, he finally shook his head a little and merely asked,

"So . . . if we're going to beat this fop, how do you propose we start?"

Eve felt a grin spread across her face. "Tonight, after I've played the harp at sunset, sneak out of the stables where you're assigned to sleep and meet me in front of the duke's study. Do you think you can do that?"

He rolled his eyes. "Sneaking out? I've been doing that since I was fourteen. What else?"

Eva considered pressing for more details about his odd remark but decided to let it go for the moment. Instead, she grinned and put her hands on her waist. "We're going to steal the Golden Goose."

8

THIS MAN HAS A PROBLEM

*E*va tapped her foot nervously as she waited in the shadow of a corner near the duke's study. *He wouldn't leave me again. He said he was going to stay. He'll stay. He'll be here.*

Of course, there were a million other reasons he might not show up. Perhaps someone had discovered his purpose for being in the duke's employ. Or the duke had had him arrested when they were apart. Or maybe he'd been caught breaking curfew. Even when the duke was gone, the servants didn't seem to consider slacking off or relaxing the rules. If anything, they worked harder.

After nearly two hours of waiting, she had nearly given up when footsteps sounded down the hall. Eva stiffened until she recognized the comforting sound of heavy boots, far different from anything the manor staff ever wore. He stopped at the study door and looked around. Eva darted out of her hiding place long enough to grab him by the sleeve, unlock the door, and drag him inside. As soon as they were in, she shut the door as quietly as possible and locked it once more.

To her relief, someone had left a low fire burning in the hearth. The light wasn't bright, but it was enough to see the hundreds of leather ledgers filling the ceiling-high bookshelves, the side tables by the chair, and even the surface of the desk itself.

Jack went up to the desk and studied the four piles that sat atop it. "This man has a problem."

"He keeps records on everything. And every ledger he owns has a double that he records at the end of the day in the off-chance it's lost." Eva looked around until she found two candles, which she lit as well and handed one to Jack. "I didn't know there was so much parchment on the entire continent, let alone in Guthward." She shook her head in disgust. "He brought me here once to show me his collection. I think he believed it would impress me."

"Did it?"

"While I find the general acquiring of information useful and even admirable in many people, there is nothing that could impress me less than records kept on how many belches different foods produce."

Jack stared at her for a long moment before finally shaking his head and looking around. "So what exactly are we looking for?" he asked as he lifted the candle.

"There's a ledger I've seen him carrying a number of times that's different from the others. It's called the Golden Goose, and I'm convinced it has to do with his plans for all those beans."

"Why are you so sure?"

She gave him a wry smile. "It's the only one he won't talk to me about. And that man will not miss any opportunity to impress me if he can help it."

"So . . ." Jack looked around the study, warily eyeing the two-foot tall stacks on the desk again. "I suppose we just begin anywhere."

Eva was trying to pick the lock on the desk drawer, and she found herself wishing she'd asked Martin for tips on breaking locks that time he'd figured it out, rather than scolding him instead.

"Whatever suits you," she said, giving up on the lock and grabbing a stack from the desk corner instead. "Only take care to return everything to the exact place you found it. The man is obsessive."

"Now what gave you that idea?" Jack sighed and lifted the closest stack from another corner of the desk.

For a long time, the only sounds were the crackling of the fire and the soft scrape of leather bindings and parchment as they skimmed the ledgers. Eva was glad for something to occupy her hands. But even as she skimmed the covers, where someone had branded a title on each, she couldn't keep the deeper parts of her mind from wandering over to the young man on the floor several feet away. It was difficult not to study the sharp angles of his chin or the way he slightly quirked his left eyebrow as he read. He was so different from the hordes of young men Sophie was always trying to introduce her to. His manner, though a bit rough, was unassuming and easy to be around. For once, she didn't feel as though she needed to act differently around him, that he was judging her, or that he even minded that she was nearly as tall as he was. And that was nice.

Finally, she could stand it no longer. "Can I ask you a question?"

Jack looked up from his pile. "I suppose."

Eva hesitated. They really should be concentrating on searching the ledgers. But weeks of being alone with only the duke and Mrs. McConnell for company had her thirsting for something more real. She wanted to talk about something other than the duke.

"You seem very good with your brothers. Well, with children really. And I was wondering how you . . ." Her voice trailed off in embarrassment, but understanding lit his eyes, and with it, what she thought looked like chagrin before he hid his face in another ledger. For a moment, she thought that perhaps she'd crossed a line and dug too deeply. Shame made her squirm as she regretted the question. But, to her surprise, a moment later he began to talk.

"After my father died, my mother always blamed me. I was the one that brought home the fever." He paused. "I was . . . I was fourteen. When I recovered, my father took ill." He shrugged. "She'd never been particularly fond of me, but after he died, she withdrew from nearly everyone and everything, including my younger brothers. If I hadn't cared for them, no one would have."

Eva stared in horror. While her family had its squabbles and imperfections, there had never been any doubt in her mind as to whether or not they had good intentions. She couldn't remember a time when she'd been sick and fewer than four or five people, with her parents leading the charge, had taken turns caring for her. They would bring soups and drinks and read her stories and fetch her anything she asked for.

"Were . . ." She had to stop and swallow before she could utter the whole sentence. "Were your parents close?"

"That's the funny thing. Not particularly." He shoved a pile of ledgers to the side and grabbed another. "But my father had promised my mother the world when they were married, and she was horribly disappointed when she realized she'd married just another farmer. She'd remind him of it every chance she got, too, that he'd told her he was going to take her to see the world." Jack stopped and stared into the fire, and Eva had to resist the urge to get off the desk where she was perched and hug him.

"She accused him of quitting the fight just before he died, and she's believed ever since that if he'd only fought harder, he would still be alive today."

"So you take care of your brothers because she—"

"She's still wandering around wishing for the life that was never really hers to begin with."

Eva shook her head to herself as she went back to reading the ledger covers. What a terrible fate, to do naught but wander about, mourning a past that never happened.

"What about your family?" He broke through her thoughts, a slight smile on his lips. "They have quite a reputation, even with those who have never met you."

She gave a dry laugh. "My family's reputation generally precedes my family wherever we go, though not for the usual reasons."

"How is that?"

"Well, to begin with, we are what most people wish they were. Fairy-blessed. Before any of us were born, my parents were wood-cutters who lived in a little cottage in the forest. My father was out chopping wood when he heard a noise. He followed it and stumbled upon a wolf in an old woman's cottage. The creature was trying to eat the old woman and her granddaughter. He killed the wolf and went back to chopping wood. The old woman followed him, however, insisting that she would find a way to pay him back."

"It sounds like a deed worth a reward," Jack said, but Eva just shook her head and gave him a wry smile.

"Apparently, the grandmother had a fairy godmother, and when she told the fairy godmother about my father's deed, the fairy godmother decided my parents should have a fairy of their own. Only, they never got a fairy godmother."

Jack looked thoughtful for a moment before his eyes grew wide. "Oh! You got that fellow—"

"We got Mortimer instead."

"What's his story?"

She snorted. "The better question would be what *isn't* his story? He's a reclusive fairy who, from what we can deduce, hates humans and would prefer to spend his time conducting fairy experiments of some kind or another. The fairy council forces him to do good deeds by giving him quotas, and if he doesn't fulfill his quotas, he's forbidden from carrying out his experiments."

"Is it just me, or are his wings rather . . ."

"Yes." Eva gave a small chuckle. "But back to his tricks, he runs around from time to time, trying to fill his quota without actually listening to anything his *godchildren* really want. Take my parents, for instance."

Jack had stopped looking through the ledgers completely and was staring at Eva in wonder. She couldn't help thinking that with his large eyes and full attention, he looked rather adorable. Not that she would tell him that. It would probably embarrass the life out of him. Martin would have dropped dead had someone told him that.

"My parents were very happy as woodcutters. They had always planned to have a small family and to enjoy their simple life in the forest. But Mortimer knew better. So against their wishes and pleas, he gave them a mansion in Torina, Astoria's capital, and made them wealthy merchants." She tried to stifle a giggle. "He also promised them many children, so six girls and one boy later, here we are. Some of the wealthiest people in Astoria, and they don't even want it."

Jack scratched the back of his head and stared at the window as though he could see through it, despite the night. "Huh," was all he finally said.

"And if that didn't make us odd enough, my parents keep a small farm on our land in the middle of the city, just because they miss the woods so much." She wrinkled her nose. "None of us children like it very much, but Rynn is rather good to go out and help them often enough."

Jack slowly picked up a pile of ledgers and placed it back on the desk, but Eva shook her head and pointed to the opposite corner.

"That one goes there. If a hair is out of place when he returns, he'll know someone's been here for sure."

"So how did you end up out here?" he asked, moving the pile where she indicated. "I assume since Mortimer is the one who found me that he's responsible for this somehow."

"Oh, he's more than a little responsible. This entire abduction is his fault." Even now, the words tasted bitter in her mouth. "I wasn't born with any sort of magic, but last year when I did a good deed, he waltzed in and decided I should be rewarded as well."

Jack had grabbed another stack of ledgers, but he stopped and tilted his head, studying her closely. "What did you do?"

Eva paused. Her parents had strictly forbidden her from telling anyone about her gift. But he knew she was responsible for the famine. What worse could happen? She was already kidnapped and being forced to use her abilities against her will, and according to the duke, would eventually be forced into matrimony as well.

Oh, hang it all.

"I gave another young woman my dress so she could have something to be married in after hers was ruined."

"So that merited what exactly? I mean, I know you do something with harps and farms, but . . ."

"I have played the harp all my life," she said, pulling a new ledger down with more force than was necessary. "So Mortimer, in his great wisdom, decided that because my parents were *wood-cutters*, he would tie my gift to a *farm*." She rolled her eyes. "Anyhow, he made it so that when I play the harp, if my heart is happy, plants will grow. If my heart is sad, they'll die." She shrugged. "The duke was unfortunately in Astoria when Mortimer gave me my *gift* and heard about it, and he was searching for me ever since, apparently."

Understanding slowly dawned on Jack's face. His mouth fell open, then he closed it, only to let it fall open again. "So you were telling the truth yesterday. You really are the—"

"Every morning, I play a song to make the duke's crops grow, and every evening, if what you say is true, I apparently play to kill everything else."

Jack put the ledger down that he had just picked up and went to stand next to the window. As he stared out into the darkness, Eva's stomach began to turn. What would he think of her now? She'd admitted her magic to him the day before. But now that he'd seen the entire truth in all its glory, would he still help her? Or would he be too angry?

For some reason, she realized Jack's disappointment in her would be far more difficult to bear than anything she'd been through so far. She couldn't let him down, too. Not after all she'd lived with over the last four weeks. To her surprise, however, a warm hand lifted her chin, and she found herself staring up into a face not only devoid of anger, but filled with compassion.

"We'll find a way to stop him and get you out . . . without letting him hurt your family," Jack said softly. "I promise."

Eva's eyes pricked at the corners. "Thank you," she whispered.

How long they stood like that, she couldn't tell. It couldn't have been more than a minute or so, but for some reason, it felt like an eternity. Finally, however, she had enough sense to take a deep, steadying breath and look down at the work before her.

"I suppose we should continue searching if we're ever going to find this ridiculous ledger." She gave a strangled laugh. "So far, I've read far more than I wish to about dachshunds, fermenting winter berries, and the art of knitting magic mittens for babies."

"This man really is mad." Jack shook his head. Then he sighed and looked up at the ceiling-high bookshelves, every single one filled completely with ledgers. "How are we going to find one single—"

Before he could finish, footsteps sounded in the hall and paused in front of the door. Jack grabbed Eva by the arm and pushed her under the desk then crawled behind it himself. The doorknob rattled, and Eva felt her stomach turn. This was it. Someone would discover them, and the duke would be informed. She would be placed under constant surveillance, locked away in her room, and the duke would use one of his horrible magic baubles to put an end to Jack. He'd probably make her watch and take notes in one of his stupid ledgers.

But to her relief, whoever it was didn't have a key, because after a moment, they resumed their walk down the hall.

"I don't think we'll be finding that goose tonight," Jack whispered. "When is he supposed to come back?"

"The day after tomorrow."

"Well." Jack stood and held out a hand. She took it, and he helped her up. "Then I suppose we shall just have to resume our goose hunt tomorrow. But in the meantime, milady." He picked up his platter and the goblets he'd tossed on the floor when they'd come in. "Would you prefer wine or cider?"

Eva giggled and slapped his arm playfully. She knew she should be disappointed that they hadn't found the ledger. With each passing day, they grew closer to whatever end the duke had planned. But beneath what should have been disappointment was also relief, and . . . dare she think it? Excitement. For the first time in her life, she was looking forward to spending an evening alone with a boy.

And, if she was going to be very truthful, a handsome one at that.

9

IT'S NOT MY FAULT YOU'RE STUMPY

" . . . *And* the next time we have a visitor of status, I do wish you would slouch a bit. It's improper to be above your superior, my harp." The duke stopped in the middle of the little bridge and gave Eva an appraising look, much like Eva's father gave the horses he considered buying at auctions. "At least your figure is decent. Slim, but rounded enough to satisfy all feminine curves." He turned back to the path and began walking again. "We'll need to make sure to lower your chair, though . . ."

"It's not my fault you're stumpy," Eva grumbled as she followed.

"What was that?"

"Those gourds over there look bumpy."

"If he refers to your *feminine curves* one more time," Jack leaned forward and hissed, "I'm going to hit him."

"What was that, my harp? You really must learn to speak up," the duke called back.

Eva plastered a false smile on her face, hoping desperately that he hadn't heard Jack's threat. "Having such a . . . keen eye for propriety must make life rather interesting."

The duke's eyes grew wide with the praise, and a beatific smile lit his face. "Though I cannot in truth say that I haven't studied social graces with zeal in order to perfect such abilities, I can say in earnest that much of my taste is all very natural to me."

Jack and Eva shared a glance. For all the duke's talk about social graces, it would be a miracle if he could manage one meal without talking with food in his mouth. Or talking at all.

But he continued talking, missing their interactions completely. "In fact," he said, stopping to study one of the bean fields at the foot of the little mountain, "it made my life rather difficult when I was a young boy and no one, with the exception of my dear mother, may she rest in peace," he stopped and placed his hand over his heart briefly, "believed or took heed of my warnings. But I can offer my services to their full extent through my elevated status now that I am master of title and property. And you, my harp, will be there by my side to learn and then pass on such social graces to our children and anyone who has the grand benefit of sitting under your tutelage."

Eva was saved from having to form a gracious response when the duke led them from one field to the next, and in his fervor on the subject, forgot to hold the gate so that she could pass through behind him. Jack leapt forward and grabbed it before the gate could swing shut on Eva. But in doing so, he tilted his platter and the goblets tipped and splashed all over her.

Eva let out a shriek as the cold liquid ran down her hair and face, but then she burst into giggles. The dress she was wearing had been requested specifically by the duke that morning, and it was her least favorite of all the gowns in her wardrobe.

"What a shame," she said, attempting to smother her laughter when the duke turned and stared at her in a horrified stupor. "Sir, I'm afraid I shall have to return to the house and change my dress." She held her sopping gown away from her legs. "I know you have business to attend to here, so my cupbearer and I will return to you as soon as we can." She turned briskly to begin walking back to the house, overjoyed to have an hour to herself, for she would certainly need a bath, when the duke followed.

"I must say, that's the third spill this week!" When neither Eva nor Jack stopped, he ran between them and blocked their path to the house. Placing his hands on his hips, he glared up at Jack. "You, James—"

"Jack."

". . . are possibly the clumsiest servant I've ever met. If you wish to continue in my services, I suggest you learn a bit of grace." He eyed Jack's uniform warily. "And perhaps how to look presentable as well."

"I really do need to change my dress," Eva said, hoping to draw the duke's attention away from Jack again. "May I go now?" How she hated that question. If she were marrying a man who was even half as pompous as the duke, she was sure he wouldn't make her ask permission to do things like leave his presence. But she had softened her demands on the duke whenever Jack was present. He already disliked the younger man, and she didn't want to give him any reasons to get rid of Jack, particularly as the duke's dismissals of his servants usually involved magic.

The duke gave a dramatic sigh and looked out at the fields longingly. "Very well, but when you are finished, I should like to see you again."

"On this particular hill?" Eva asked.

"No, meet me in my study. I have some material I should like for you to read."

Eva nodded and turned to go. As she went, though, her heart sank lower than it had been in weeks.

In the four weeks since Jack had arrived, Eva felt as though she had rediscovered herself. Though she still played the unwilling fiancée, bowing to the duke's wishes grudgingly so as not to endanger those around her, she knew that as soon as the duke was gone on another two- or three-day trip, she would once again get a taste of what it felt like to be herself. Jack, though somewhat unlikely to bathe on a regular basis and fairly inept in the realm of the social graces that the duke so highly favored, was completely and utterly without pretense. Never had Eva felt so comfortable around another person that she wasn't related to. So if obeying the duke meant keeping Jack around for a little longer, that was a price Eva was willing to pay.

If she was truly honest with herself, she was forced to admit that she was actually enjoying life in a way she hadn't in over a year. Though Jack was supposed to be silent whenever he posed as her attendant, he always found little ways to remind her that he was there, ways that would have never even crossed the duke's mind. For instance, a rainstorm of epic proportions had come several weeks earlier. Eva had requested leave from their usual walk the next morning because of the mud, but the duke insisted that they continue with their exercise, rain or none. And if that wasn't bad enough, he also insisted that she wear the most ridiculous high-heeled shoes she owned.

Not once on their walk had the duke turned to see how she fared. Instead, he waxed long about himself, only stopping to chide her when her progress grew too slow for his liking. Jack, on the other hand, had been there with a steady arm every time she had slipped and fallen. And as soon as they were out of sight of the duke once they reached the house, he had let her lean on him all the way up to her room to nurse the ankle she had twisted during one of her falls.

She had also found immense comfort in knowing she wasn't completely insane whenever the duke made ridiculous requests or spent an excessive amount of time critiquing her person. Had she been alone, Eva might have been tempted to believe him after hundreds of such vexing sessions as the duke told her how she really ought to present herself. How inadequate she was. How he wished her to be shorter or more delicate or to have longer eyelashes.

The insults had stung at first, and during her first three weeks alone at the duke's home, she had fallen into danger of beginning to entertain questions as to whether she really did need better features. But since Jack had come, all she had to do was turn around for a fleeting glance at her friend, and with the roll of his eyes or the slight furrow of his brow, she knew that she really wasn't as bad off as the duke's lectures made her sound.

There were many times, unfortunately, that Jack couldn't be with her to lessen the verbal blows of her captor. Whenever the duke was not on one of his mysterious trips, he generally insisted that Eva stay in his study with him while he wrote in his ledgers and explained his notes in great detail. Jack was also prohibited from leaving the outdoor sleeping situation, as were all servants and workers, whenever Eva played her harp. And though Jack's presence at first had merely been a breath of fresh air, a subtle reminder of the world outside, Eva found herself craving his attention more and more with each passing day. She sometimes wished to stumble, simply so she could feel the warmth of his steady hand whenever he reached out to catch her, and whenever the duke insisted on holding her hand and pleading for just a small kiss, she couldn't help wondering if she would have refused so readily if Jack had been the one to ask.

"Are you feeling well?"

"What?" Eva looked up and realized Jack had asked her a question. They were almost to the house, and she had wasted the majority of their precious time alone brooding.

"You look a bit pale," Jack said, taking her gently by the arm and turning her to face him. "I asked if you're feeling well." He raised the back of his hand and placed it gently against her cheek. "You feel a bit warm."

"Oh," Eva tried to sound lighthearted as she resumed her walk back to the house. "For not having a particularly attentive mother, you seem well adept at assessing the health of others."

Jack gave her a wan smile as he followed her. "You forget, I have two little brothers. While my mother doesn't seem to dislike them the way she does me, she was never one to coddle any of us once we were past infancy." A shadow flitted across his face, but it was gone so quickly Eva wasn't sure if it had really even been there. "My father, however," his voice softened, "was very attentive up until the day he died."

Eva resisted the urge to take his hand and squeeze it, and instead satisfied herself with giving his shoulder an awkward pat as they walked.

"I suppose I'm getting tired of the charade," she said. "We're no closer to discovering his plans, and I fear his goals are nearing completion." She stopped and looked up at the big house as they moved beneath its shade. The noon sun was growing rather hot, and her dress was sticky with the residue of Jack's spilled goblets. She glanced around to make sure no one was watching before she stepped closer and pitched her voice low. "I'm scared, Jack. What do we do if—"

"We'll find a way, Eva." He placed a callused hand on her shoulder and gently squeezed. "I'm not going to leave you to him. I promise."

"What about your brothers?" she whispered. "I don't know how much longer this will take."

"Mortimer said he would take care of them until I was finished here. It was part of the deal." He glanced around and nodded at the house. "We'd better keep moving before someone spots us."

He was right. They'd stayed out talking too long already. Eva sighed and headed toward the door.

"What has you so worried all of a sudden?" he asked when they found the inner hall clear of servants.

"I suppose it's this meeting he wants." She shook her head as they turned a corner. "Every time he—" She paused and Jack held up his platter to a proper height as two young servants passed them. They only spoke again when the servants were long gone. Unfortunately, they were close to Eva's room by then.

"Every time he wants to speak with me alone, I just *know* he's going to have a wedding date. Then we'll be too late, and he'll get everything he wants after all." They came to a stop outside Eva's door. Eva wrapped her arms around herself and shivered. "I wish Rynn were here. She would know what to do."

Jack frowned and rubbed his neck thoughtfully with his free hand. "Well," he finally said, "whatever he says, I'll be right there behind you, and that means we'll be one step ahead this time."

Eva tapped his nose with her finger and gave him a sad smile. "You're sweet. But I get the unfortunate suspicion that this is one meeting he'll want to have alone."

∾

An hour later, after a bath had been drawn and her clothes and shoes had been changed, Eva stood dutifully in the duke's study. What seemed like such a cozy, comfortable room on the nights when Eva and Jack searched for the mysterious Golden Goose ledger felt cold and inhospitable during the day. Or maybe it was just because the duke was present. The only comfort she could find was in Jack's silent presence behind her. Even if he was only a servant, and a false one at that, he was there.

The duke walked in with an air of confidence, his idiotic smile spread from ear to ear. He paused on the way to his desk and examined Eva with his beady gaze. When she'd first come to the manor, it had unnerved her the way his eyes examined her person, always looking for a runaway lock of hair or a wrinkle that had been put in the skirt of her dress, but it no longer got under her skin. One day, she promised herself, the tides would turn, and without endangering Jack or anyone else, she would be able to meet his critical stare with a good hard cuff to those sickly pale cheeks. Until then, however, she simply satisfied herself with imagining it over and over again in her head.

"Quite decent," he finally said, nodding slowly at her gown. "While I'm partial to the dress you were wearing this morning, I'm surprisingly fond of this one as well. It makes you look shorter."

Out of the corner of her eye, Eva saw Jack's hands flex.

"What exactly was it that you called me here for?" Eva asked before Jack could get himself into trouble. She was shocked the duke had allowed him to remain even this long.

"Ah, yes." The duke went around to the other side of his desk and picked up a book. After blowing a layer of dust off the top, he walked back and handed it to Eva. "While I have enjoyed our exercise and concurrent discourse, I have decided that with the pinnacle of our plans drawing nearer, it's high time that you become familiar with your future duties."

"Duties?"

"Your duties as queen, of course."

Eva looked down at the book in her hands. She didn't dare open it yet, but the sheer thickness of the volume was mildly terrifying. Flurries of angst, much like the flurries in a winter snowstorm, began swirling in her gut. Were they really so close to the end of his plans already? She had hoped for more time, the remainder of the summer at least, before she had to make a decision on what to do regarding the duke. Determined not to let her anxiety get the better of her, however, Eva licked her lips and decided to take advantage of the situation as best she could.

"When you say queen," she said slowly, "you really mean to say that . . ." Her mind worked as fast as it could trying to come up with another way to draw his secrets out of him. "You mean you want me to marry the king?" She knew better, of course. But he already thought her a dunce compared to his impressive intellect. She might as well use this against him, anything to work those secrets out of his tight little grasp.

As she'd expected, the duke put his head in his hands and rubbed his eyes. "There are some days, my harp—"

"I told you not to call me that."

" . . . when I wonder just how many ways your parents neglected your education and the building up of your intellect. Why else would I have spent all this time writing you poems and stories and singing the songs of my own creation?"

Oh, the songs. Those terrible, terrible songs. Jack had once aptly likened them to a cow attempting to sing.

"But you are only second in line for the throne. King Eston is only thirty and five years, and from what I hear, in quite good health. He still has much time to find a wife and have children."

"True as that may be, my cousin has little desire to raise a family. He's too busy waltzing around with whatever woman he wishes. Wooing for fun, rather than for keeps, as he likes to say. And it's causing no small amount of concern amongst the nobles." He stopped his pacing and gave her a fierce smirk. "Believe me when I say that our chances of gaining the throne naturally are quite good. And if all goes according to plan, they will be even better."

He paused and rubbed a finger on one of the bookshelves, his brow momentarily creasing when he examined his finger. "That, of course, brings us back to the topic of your education. And as you are obviously lacking in an understanding of the finer points of etiquette and the responsibilities of queen, I want you to have this book read by supper of two days henceforth."

Eva gaped at the book. "You want me to read *this* in two days?" Her voice sounded shrill even in her own ears. "I can't read that fast—"

"You can, and you will." He arched a single brow, making his puffy face look even more like that of a pigeon. "And should I find you struggling with distractions . . ." He beckoned for Jack to come near. Jack walked stiffly to stand at the duke's side, refusing to take his eyes off the wall behind Eva. His jaw muscles twitched as the duke reached up and took one of the goblets for himself, drinking deeply before replacing it. "I will have such distractions removed without warning." He folded his hands and smiled. "Do I make myself clear?"

It was all Eva could do to nod and walk from the room without allowing her trembling to overtake her.

10

YOU'RE NONE OF THOSE THINGS

*J*ack had the nearly overwhelming urge to hurl one of the goblets at the duke's head, but instead he forced himself to maintain his servant's posture as he followed Eva out of the study.

Her own posture was flawless, and she held her head high, but he didn't miss the shudder of her shoulders as they turned the corner. She somehow kept the proud bearing, though, until she had led them out of the house completely and into the rose garden. Once they were hidden from view of the house by a trellis covered in red climbing roses, she sank to her knees. A single tear ran down her cheek, followed by another and another until she shook with violent, silent sobs.

Jack had never felt so helpless.

A rush of emotions swept him like a tornado, sucking him in and jerking his heart around as Eva held her face in her hands, her shoulders curved inward as she cried. Anger was first, anger like he hadn't felt before. Despite all the acts Eva had to put on daily, she still treated the duke far better than he deserved. She was too polite not to. Even her insults, whether whispered or told to his face, weren't nearly as vile as the duke had earned.

Still, she had born his comments well, absurd as they tended to be. The duke's cowardly cuts and critiques hadn't bothered her. Or at least, Jack thought they hadn't. But now he could see that all the insults the duke liked to heap upon her, all the little ways he found to criticize her over the course of the summer were starting to chip away at the confidence she somehow maintained whenever the duke was present. This alarmed him more than he wanted to admit. Eva was the last person who should be weeping on the ground, and the duke should be the last person with the power to break her.

The whole situation was utterly wrong.

Jack reached out a hand, but it took him several failed attempts before he mustered up enough courage to stiffly pat her on the head.

"You . . . you can't listen to him," he said. "He's trying to hurt you. He just wants to knock you down so you'll have to look up to him."

Eva sniffed and looked up at Jack, her tear-stained cheeks making her brown eyes look even larger than usual. As she gazed at him, Jack found himself wishing to wipe the tears away with his hands and to pull her into a deep embrace the way his father had once done for him. If only he could will the hurt away from the gentle creature before him.

But would she welcome such a touch? Or would she think he was simply trying to manipulate her, too?

Instead, he satisfied himself with sitting beside her on the ground, making sure their knees didn't touch.

"I haven't always been this much of a coward," she sniffed, wiping her face on her sleeve.

"I never thought you were a coward."

"But I have been." Eva let out a shuddering sigh as she fingered the book. "Here I am with magic so powerful it's somehow affecting all of Guthward, and I can't bring myself to use it against him." She shrugged. "My siblings were always trying to get me to be more adventurous. 'Eva, just try! The junbon's sour, but it's good!'

'Eva, wear the red dress!' 'Eva, just give the boy a chance and dance with him!'" She let out a shaky laugh as she idly flipped the pages. "If you asked my younger sister Sophie, you'd think I'd never done anything worth doing in my life that wasn't told me."

Jack just listened, not sure he was really qualified to comment. He didn't know what a junbon was, but he *was* sure he would like to see her in a red dress. And for some reason, he really, really hoped she hadn't given the boy a chance, whoever he was.

"But I've never really *lived*!" she continued, the tears beginning to fall once again. "And just when I was going to, Mortimer had to swoop in and ruin it all!"

Jack thought for a moment. "If you had the chance . . . to do whatever you wanted, I mean, what . . . what would you do?"

She swallowed, and he handed her a goblet, for once glad he had to carry the awful tray with him wherever he went. When she'd finished drinking, she handed it back to him and stared up into the white cottony clouds that floated above.

"Before Mortimer gave me the magic, I was supposed to be the head harpist at the Winter Ball. I'd dreamed about it for years." Her eyes grew distant, and a small smile appeared between her tear-stained cheeks. "It's one of the grandest compliments any musician can be given, and I'd practiced for years just to be invited." She looked back down at the book. "Music brings me joy. Or it used to, at least. I had hoped, one day after some performing, to teach music as well as play. To get married and have a family. Children and music are the two things that make me happiest in this world." Her timid smile disappeared again. "But if the duke gets his way, I'll be playing music on command for the rest of my days."

They were quiet for a long time. As the noon sun took on its afternoon glow, Jack was very aware of the delicate hand that was only inches from his. He stared at it longingly out of the corner of his eye. Did he dare reach out and take it?

"A schoolmaster," he said instead.

She looked up, those doe-like eyes searching his once more. "What?"

"You said you wanted to be a musician. I wanted to be a schoolmaster."

She stared at him, so he went on before he could reconsider his choice to embarrass himself by speaking.

"Before my father died, I had the chance to attend school long enough to learn how to read simple things and do basic arithmetic. I even won a counting contest once." He smiled at the memory, remembering how proud he had been of the little jar of peach preserves he'd won and taken home to present his mother with. She'd grumbled about disliking peaches, but his father had been ecstatic.

"Why did you stop?" Eva asked.

"I didn't want to. But after my father died, my mother said I had to be the man around the house. Which meant that at age fourteen, I was running the farm by myself." He shook his head. "While I attended school, the schoolmaster allowed me to help the younger students learn. That became my favorite part of the day. I realized quickly that I wanted nothing more than to have my own school-house when I grew older. I would teach them, and life would be grand. But when my mother took me out of school, I knew I would never get to teach." When he looked at Eva, she appeared horrified.

"Why not?"

"What town is going to choose a schoolmaster who never finished school himself? I didn't even complete my basic learning, let alone study at a university."

When he looked up again, to his surprise, all of the sorrow had fled Eva's face. And it had been replaced with a nearly terrifying determination.

"What's stopping you now?" She sat straighter. "Why shouldn't you have a chance? You're obviously intelligent enough, and you're wonderful with children!"

He smiled, his cheeks heating a bit at the praise. "As kind as that is of you to say, I'm afraid it's not that simple. My brothers aren't old enough to run the farm on their own yet, and won't be for a while. And even then, I would still need more money than I've ever made in my life." He let out a dry chuckle. "Farming isn't exactly the way to make an easy fortune. Besides, my mother owns the coin we make, and she certainly won't be sending me any, anytime soon."

"Oh." Eva's shoulders slumped again.

"What did you do?" he asked, hoping to keep her mind from returning to that morning.

"What did I do?"

"You said you did a good deed and Mortimer rewarded you."

"Oh." She waved a hand. "It wasn't a deed worth a reward." Then she scoffed. "And what makes it even worse is that my sisters warned me not to. But I didn't listen."

"Why does he give rewards out at all? Especially if you hate them so?"

"Mortimer has a bad habit of falling behind on his wish-granting. So he shows up at random times and bestows gifts on whomever he can find, whether they want the gifts or not." She chuckled softly. "Our first twins, Martin and Ellie, were given the gift of beauty at birth. It drives Ellie mad because that's all anyone sees when they look at her. Martin whines that he looks like a girl. Sophie, the sister immediately my junior, always knows what time it is, and Penny, one of our youngest twins, has amethyst eyes." Her smile faded. "I thought I could pass the dress off and he wouldn't know. I suppose that was rather naive now that I think about it."

"I think it was pretty brave."

"What?" She looked up at him, eyes still red at the corners.

"I mean it." He shifted to face her. "You knew what you were risking, and yet you took the chance on being kind. So I don't think you can really say you aren't brave."

She stared at him for a long minute. What she saw, he wished he knew. Or perhaps he didn't. All he knew was that the longer he stared into the warm depths of her gaze, the more he wanted to continue. What would it feel like to reach out and touch her cheek? To take her hand?

He couldn't tell just how long they sat that way, staring at one another wordlessly, but eventually, she blinked a few times and looked up at the sky.

"Well, if I'm to have any of this read in the next two days, I suppose I should begin soon." She stood and began slowly back down the winding path. Jack stood, too, gathering his platter and goblets, both of which were now empty, and followed. Before they left the garden, however, he reached out and grabbed her hand. She turned to look at him with questioning eyes.

"You're beautiful, you know." Why did his voice sound so thick?

Her eyes somehow grew even wider, and he couldn't tell if it was from shock at the touch or embarrassment at the statement. So he decided to finish before the remnants of his nerve could flee him.

"Don't let him make you feel ugly or stupid or inadequate. Because you're none of those things." He paused, his gaze dropping to where he still held her hand. "Any real man could see that."

He let her hand go, but for a split second, he was rather sure she had squeezed his back.

11

DON'T BE SORRY

"What exactly did the duke threaten me with if I don't finish this by tomorrow?" Eva glared at the book as she turned another page.

Jack looked up from the ledger he was holding. "That he would remove me, if I recall correctly."

Eva made a scoffing sound but went back to reading. A few minutes later, Jack started chuckling. She looked up from her page.

"What is it?"

He grinned. "Is it really that bad?"

"It's like I'm opening my head and dumping piles of sand inside on purpose. But why do you ask?"

"Since you sat down to read, you've let out a sigh every thirty seconds or so."

"It's awful," she groaned, straightening her legs. It really wasn't a very ladylike way to sit, but she was tired and frustrated, and the book only seemed to get longer the more she read. Sometimes, a girl just had to sit on the floor and stretch. Then she sat up a little straighter. "You doubt me? Listen to this." She cleared her throat. "If the queen wishes for something to eat between meals, she shall ring a bell or other mechanism to garner the attention of her inferiors. Shouting, however, is strictly forbidden. Going to the kitchens personally is even less appropriate. If one is in the unfortunate position of having a lazy maidservant or even lazier ladies-in-waiting that do not come when the bell is rung, it is permissible to obtain their attentions through a low call."

"That is . . . specific," Jack said, shaking his head. "Who writes this tripe?"

"I can guarantee you it wasn't a queen. Or even a woman." Eva scowled.

"For all his insistence on propriety, he does know he's the rudest, crassest, most slovenly creature on the face of the earth, correct? Particularly when he's eating."

"I doubt it. Listen, it gets worse. 'Once a reliable source for fetching the food has been found, the food itself should be cautiously chosen. There shall be no chocolate or sweets. Neither shall a queen indulge in any sorts of meat between meals, but rather, she shall tastefully enjoy a prepared square of barley or some . . . '" Eva squinted at the page. That couldn't be right. "Broth?"

Jack looked up from the ledgers again, but this time he looked horrified. "Broth? If you're hungry?"

" . . . lest," Eva continued reading, "the queen become stout and uncomely because of overindulging—"

"Let me see that."

The book disappeared from her hands, and Jack, who was standing above her, leafed through it with a frown. "I've never heard of anything so ridiculous. Who acts like this?"

"I met the queen of Astoria once when I was performing at a season festival, and she was absolutely nothing like a queen is described in this book."

"Well," Jack said, closing the book with a thump, "all I can say is that we'd better stop the duke if you'd like to escape starvation and live past the age of twenty."

Though she knew he'd meant it as a joke, Eva felt her heart fall.

"What is it?" The smirk left his face.

She shook her head. "I might finish this book by tomorrow, but it's only a matter of time before he does it again. And again."

"What do you mean?"

"For the rest of his existence, he'll use everything I love against me. He knows where my family lives. And eventually, if he gets his way," she made a face, "eventually, our children . . ." She looked at Jack. "You're only the beginning."

Jack's face had darkened at the mention of children, but then he looked surprised, and it took a moment for Eva to realize why.

Everything she loved began with him.

She hadn't meant to say she loved him. She hadn't even been aware of it. But now that she considered how much leverage the duke had over her . . .

The power he held by threatening Jack was far more than she had ever meant for it to be. Had the duke spoken of hurting Jack at the beginning of his stay at the mansion, Eva would have been horrified. Having the blood of anyone on her conscience would have made her sick.

But in the past four weeks, he had become so much more than *just anyone*. He had dried her tears, followed her around as a servant, and been a constant comforting presence. Every morning, she was able to play a song of joy because she knew she had something to look forward to that day, and each night, her song of sorrow wasn't so sad because she knew the next day would hold companionship. He didn't have to stay. He could have left her anytime and gone to take his brothers far away, and she wouldn't have held it against him. And yet, he *had* stayed. And continued to search and comfort and calm her. And he thought she was beautiful.

When was the last time someone had called her beautiful? Probably the day she'd tried on the blue dress, over a year before.

But . . . did he feel the same way about her? Had she just crossed a line she couldn't take back?

"Jack," she said, twisting her hands and staring at the ground, "I didn't mean—"

"Hold on."

She looked up to see him squinting at the corner of the book-shelf, just beside the door. She followed his gaze down to see a single ledger barely out of line with the others. Jack strode over to the shelf and bent to pick it up. When he did, his jaw dropped. He held it up for her to read, and Eva nearly collapsed.

On the front of the ledger, burned into the leather, were the words *Golden Goose*.

Revelations of emotion temporarily forgotten, Eva hopped up and ran to see. But as she did, voices sounded in the hall. To her horror, the loudest belonged to the duke.

" . . . must have forgotten it in my study."

Eva and Jack sprinted to the desk and began shoving ledgers back into the places they'd pulled them from. The doorknob began to turn, but it caught on the lock. Eva threw Jack a look of panic.

"Are you sure you left it in here, my lord?" Mrs. McConnell's muffled voice came through. "You were in your chambers last before you left."

"I would appreciate you not questioning my memory, which, as you know, is flawless." The key slid into the lock, and Jack grabbed Eva and shoved her behind the right curtain, then leapt behind the left. Eva sent up a prayer of thanks that the curtains reached to the floor as the door clicked open and footsteps padded in. Her heart pounded in her stomach as she listened for the cry of discovery that would doom both her and Jack forever.

Each second was an eternity. Would he be able to tell that they'd moved anything? She had been fairly certain that she and Jack had put everything back where they'd found it, but now that the silence stretched on, she wasn't so sure.

"Where in the blazes . . . Oh. Here it is. Funny, this is the double. I don't recall placing it here."

"A servant might have moved it to dust, sir," Mrs. McConnell said.

Bless her, Eva thought as she closed her eyes. Her relief was short-lived, however, when she heard the heavier set of footsteps come to a stop just on the other side of the curtain. She held her breath. What if this was it? What would he do if he discovered them?

After waiting for what felt like hours, the footsteps finally moved back toward the door. "Even with the delay," the duke said, "I should back by noon tomorrow. Proceed with the preparations for the dinner party as planned."

"Yes, my lord," Mrs. McConnell said, shutting the door behind her. Neither Eva nor Jack moved until the lock had clicked shut and both sets of footsteps had retreated down the hall and disappeared. Eva let out the breath she'd been holding and peeked out of the curtain. Jack was doing the same.

"That was close!" he said, his eyes bright. "I thought he had us for sure."

"So did I." Eva let out a nervous chuckle as she stepped out of her hiding place. "But we didn't get to see the plans. He took them."

"That he did."

"So why do you still look so happy?" Eva asked.

"Because," Jack said, sweeping into a deep bow, "aside from narrowly escaping discovery and what would have been our sure doom, we now know where he keeps the Golden Goose . . . or its double, or whatever that was. And since he's coming home tomorrow—"

"We'll know where to look!" Eva hopped up and down, clapping. "I know I can come up with an excuse to get into the study some-time when he's not here. I can forget something on purpose in here the next time he calls me, and then I can insist on returning to fetch whatever I've—"

Before she could continue to plot, however, Jack had swept her up in his arms and placed a kiss right on her lips.

The kiss wasn't long, nor was it passionate. Only a peck really. But almost as soon as he had done it, Jack let go of her hand and took a few steps back. His face was nearly the color of a tomato.

"I . . . I'm sorry." His smile was gone, and his eyes were wide with alarm. He scratched his neck and stared at the floor. "I just got carried away in the moment, I guess."

But Eva could only smile. Inside, she was singing. Never had a boy kissed her before. She wasn't sure if any had ever even wanted to. But in that brief moment of bliss, the joy of his kiss was infectious. She had felt the smile on his lips as they'd touched hers, and it made her want to smile back.

"Don't be sorry," she said shyly.

His eyes finally left the floor, and when he met her gaze, his grin slowly returned.

"Alright then," he said in a low voice. "I won't."

YOU'LL NEED NOTHING SHORT OF A MIRACLE

*J*ack had to remind himself again and again to remain still and keep his eyes forward like a good servant should. It was the duke's dinner party after all, and certainly not the place to be discovered snooping. But, he had grumbled to Eva earlier that day, he was not a good servant. He wasn't even a servant. At which point, Eva had smugly reminded him that he had been paid just earlier that week for waiting on her hand and foot. And he had accepted the payment without complaint then. Which, she had smirked, made him a servant.

The real servant was Eva, though. At the mercy of the duke's beck and call, she didn't even have a say in what was served for dinner. This evening, for instance, one of the main courses was ham covered in beets. Eva hated beets, and she had told the duke so at least five times. They gave her mouth a rash every time she ate them. But every time she made her objection, the duke would only respond with some condescending cut, and beets would appear on not just one dish, but all of them the next meal. The last time this had happened, Jack had nearly marched up to the duke's bedchamber to give him a good thrashing. Instead, however, he'd gone in search for Mrs. McConnell for some aloe for Eva's mouth.

A kitchen maid walked past Jack's corner carrying a covered platter that smelled strongly of mouth-watering herbs, and then Jack had to really work on keeping his focus sharp and not on the food. The food he and the other temporary workers, such as the field laborers and those that fed them, were given wasn't necessarily bad, particularly considering that the rest of the kingdom was eating beans day and night. But compared to the porridge he and the others got every morning and the two meals of bread, milk, and stewed fruits and vegetables, he wasn't sure his stomach had ever grumbled so much at the smell of a simple seasoned soup

He held his platter of goblets higher when he finally heard the voices and footsteps of Eva, the duke, and those he assumed to be the duke's guests. If keeping his focus off the food had been difficult, however, it was nothing compared to the hardship he faced when Eva walked into the room.

Though her dress was another horrid shade of green, Eva made the gown look stunning. Cut to hang off the shoulders, the shiny fabric fell gently below her collarbone, where it exploded into beaded swirls that looked like roses that tapered down to her waist. Just below her waist, the skirt's many layers of some even shinier material that Jack didn't know the name of reached down to the ground like the arms of a weeping willow. And—Jack nearly smirked—it made her look even taller than usual. Lean muscled arms were poised gracefully at her sides, and though the duke held one of them, Jack could see she was making a great effort to touch him as little as possible. Still, even the few inches of gloved skin that the duke was privileged to hold made Jack's stomach turn. He should be escorting her, not that horrid little dingleberry.

Behind Eva and the duke walked six other individuals. A short, stout man with hair that was obviously not his, then a young dark-haired woman draped in furs, her expression signaling the intelligence of a mop. Her eyes were trained solely on the duke, though every few steps she would briefly glare daggers at Eva's back. Another woman with graying hair and sharp, beady eyes came next, and she was followed by an older couple that clutched one another's arms and watched everything with suspicion. Then came a bland-faced gentleman with no visible neck and very little chin. All of the guests were dressed in clothes finer than anything anyone in Jack's village wore, and when they got to the table, they looked around as though such fare, dozens and dozens of silver platters and dishes, were a daily occurrence.

"My friends," the duke began when they were all standing beside their assigned seats, "I offer you the bounty of my home."

"Quite generous of you," the wife of the older couple said, quirking an eyebrow, "particularly as the rest of the kingdom must order its food from across the border now."

"Yes," said her husband, frowning. "It would be a relief if we knew how to replicate your efforts in order to better feed those who depend on us."

Though Jack had first assumed a dislike of everyone fool enough to associate themselves with the duke, he decided that this couple might not be quite so awful.

"All in good time." The duke smiled and gestured to their chairs. Servants appeared out of the shadows and pulled the chairs out for the guests, and then pushed them back in once they were seated. Jack resisted the urge to glare at the servant who pushed Eva's chair in for her. That was *his* job.

"I don't mean to be rude," the woman with the pinched mouth said, "but this supper is unusually early." She glanced outside. "We're hardly done with the afternoon."

"My betrothed and I," the duke patted Eva's head, not unlike one might do to a dog, "have work to get to, unfortunately, and it must be done by dusk. I hope you don't mind."

"So, Carlton," the short, stout gentleman said as he dumped salt into his soup, "what's this about? Last I heard, you're handing out beans, and now you surprise us with this to sup on." He slurped down a mouthful and his eyes grew wide. "And it tastes fresh enough not to have been brought in from elsewhere."

"What you are eating, my dear judge," the duke said after slurping his soup, "is all from my lands. The livestock, the poultry, the grains, milk, and produce were all grown and prepared here."

"But how?" The sharp-eyed woman studied her bowl. "We've all had to pay to bring food in."

It was a moment before the duke spoke. He wiped his mouth and stared at his bowl for a moment before looking up at everyone with a smile. "What do you all know of the king's stance on magic?"

"I asked him such last week," the bland-faced gentleman said. "He says it's unnecessary and creates too many complications."

"And how has this simple life . . . this existence without magic, helped him combat our strange famine?" the duke asked.

The guests exchanged glances.

"I thought practicing magic was difficult in Guthward," the elderly husband said. "Our clay is good for growing, but it also blocks much of the magic that's needed to flow through the ground . . . or something to that effect."

The duke nodded. "You are correct, Baron. But suppose I had found a way to make the land fertile again." The duke stood and began to walk slowly around the table, coming to stop between the woman glaring at Eva and the judge. "And then suppose," he leaned forward, "I had gone to the king and told him I have a way to end the famine. What would you say the king's response should be?"

For a long moment, no one spoke. And even Jack understood why. Speaking in hypothetical situations was innocent enough, but when the topic turned to discussing the king, it was only wise to be careful.

Finally, the dark-haired young woman spoke, her voice tentative. "Wouldn't he be . . . relieved?"

"You would think so." The duke nodded and continued his walk around the table. "But again, suppose the king be not thrilled, and even that he dismissed the topic altogether, stating that his best advisers and farmers would come up with a way to fix the soil. Tell me," he stopped behind his seat at the head of the table, "what the moral obligation would be then, of the one who knew how to fix the problem? Would it be correct to allow the king to continue to flounder with dead crops, or would it be the righteous thing to disobey the king by moving forward with an assurance to fix the crops, but risk angering the crown at the same time?"

"What are you getting at, Carlton?" The baron stopped eating and frowned.

"Answer the question first. Is it the moral choice to disobey the king and provide for the kingdom, or to obey the king and watch children and babies risk starvation?"

None of the guests, even the one who had been practically drooling over the duke a moment before, looked comfortable. Eva didn't even raise her head enough for Jack to try to make out her expression. He wondered if her submissive position had been learned in that stupid book with all its rules, or whether she wanted nothing to do with the situation at hand. The bland-faced man opened and closed his mouth as though to speak several times without actually saying anything, and the older couple pushed their food around their plates. To Jack's surprise, however, it was finally the judge that spoke.

"If one wished to change the law regarding magic," he said slowly, "one would need to assume the title of king without being arrested for treason for going against the crown's edicts."

"Treason is a bit strong for a simple act of disobedience, don't you think?" The dark-haired woman frowned.

"Not when it comes to magic." The judge shook his head. "The king has very staunch opinions on the matter."

"Well, we can't just wait for the king to die!"

Everyone, including Eva, turned and looked at the woman in her forties, slightly scandalized expressions on their faces.

"Oh, don't pretend you aren't thinking the same thing!" She began buttering her bread fiercely. "King Eston is thirty-five, and without any children to drive him to an early grave, we can't simply wait this drought out in hopes that something changes before he dies!"

"She brings up a good point," the bland-faced man said, looking down at the plate of fish a servant had just placed before him. "The king has no children and seems to have very little interest in ever producing any . . . even an illegitimate one. He refuses to consider magic as an alternative to this drought, and with every second we waste, more people are fleeing the kingdom than ever." He looked at the judge. "Surely there must be a way to make him see sense."

"There is no legal way to force a king to act." The judge shook his head.

"There is, however, no need to fret, my dear countess," the duke said with a slight smile. "For there is yet another option, wouldn't you say, Your Honor?"

"Well," the judge said, looking around once again and reluctantly putting down the roll he'd been studying, "there is technically one way to replace him with someone who would allow magic."

The table went silent. The guests stopped with food halfway to their mouths, and even the servants froze and stared. But the duke kept that ridiculous grin and stood a little taller.

Eva gestured for Jack. He brought her the tray, and she took a much longer sip from her special goblet than usual.

"Imagine that there was someone who was willing to do what it took to end this famine. And that he even had proof that he knew how to do so." The duke moved to stand behind Eva and placed his hands firmly on her shoulders. "And that he also was engaged to a woman of youth and strength who could bear him many, many children in order to avoid the tragedy of never having an heir."

Jack resisted the sudden urge to gag. Even more, however, he had to resist the urge to forcefully remove the duke's puffy hands from Eva's bare shoulders.

"Your Honor," the duke said, looking at the judge once more, "how would one go about that?"

The judge frowned and rubbed his chin. "Guthward's bylaws," he said carefully, "allow a close relative of the king to replace him, should the vast majority of the peerage call for the selection of a more fitting ruler in his place. But," he said in a lower voice, "the peerage would have to be utterly convinced that the replacement would be superior to the king in every manner. In short, they would need to view the king as a sort of villain before replacing him. It's only been done once in Guthwardian history, and even then, it nearly tore the kingdom apart."

"But King Eston has been good to us!" the old woman exclaimed. "He has dropped all taxes until our crops grow again! And he's always been good to listen to even the most lowly citizen who has sought his aid."

"I'm not sure what you're at, Carlton," the baron glared at the duke, "but you won't have our vote. Eston is a good king."

Jack's heart fell a little as the duke's mouth curved up at the corners. Should the duke get his way, Jack was sure the kindly old couple would be the first of the nobility to disappear, along with anyone who stood with them.

"Very well," the duke finally said, taking his seat and attacking his food with great gusto. "Now, Bentley," he said, turning to the earl. "I heard that you enjoy poetry. I'm a bit of a poet myself."

The duke's disgusting smile didn't falter for the rest of the meal, particularly as he regaled his guests with pieces of his own crass poetry, all spoken between bites of fish, where everyone could see the food rolling around in his mouth.

For all the duke's insistence on Eva memorizing her court manners, little Larry had better table manners.

Once they escaped his poetry, lighter topics were discussed for the remainder of the dinner. Eva, however, hardly ate. And once, just once, Jack thought he saw a single tear roll down her cheek and into her dish. The other nobles, for that's what Jack assumed the rest of them to be, sent her curious, or jealous, looks for the rest of the meal, but interestingly enough, the only two willing to address her directly were the baron and his wife. And every time she tried to answer, the duke would find a way to enter that conversation as well.

It wasn't until hours later, when the guests were finally preparing to leave, that anyone dared to bring up the subject of magic again. But the sharp-eyed woman, who Jack had discovered was a countess, paused on the threshold of the great dining room and turned to the duke.

"You never told us just how you've managed to keep your estate running so well." She glanced around furtively. "Or food growing in your fields."

"Ah, madame," the duke bowed with a flourish, "that's a secret you'll have to wait for until my wedding, I'm afraid."

Eva stiffened.

"Just suffice it to say for now that magic is going to save our people. Magic with a power like you've never seen before."

"Careful."

Jack jumped at the warning whispered in his ear. He turned to find Mrs. McConnell beside him in the shadows.

"Why?" he asked.

"I don't know what you're up to, but I know you're in love with the girl."

Jack couldn't answer, only stare.

As if to congratulate herself on being right, Mrs. McConnell nodded. "The duke sees that girl as his prize, and you'll need nothing short of a miracle to separate that man from his prey."

WHEN YOUR PALMS GET SWEATY, YOU MUST BE IN LOVE

*A*s they bid farewell to their guests, Eva wanted nothing more than to run into her room, slam the door, and hide under her covers for the rest of eternity. Surviving the evening without breaking down into tears or throwing something at the duke's head had taken every piece of stage training she had ever learned with the harp. Breathing practice to overcome the jitters in her stomach. Pretending she had a stick tied to the back of her neck to keep her eyes forward and her chin up as she greeted their guests and then bid them farewell, hoping that each one might see the desperate plea in her eyes, begging them to see that she was a prisoner and needed to escape.

And she had been mostly successful. Mostly.

But as the evening had gone on, she got the distinct feeling that no matter what the rest of the nobles in the dining room thought, the duke held all the power in his puffy little hands.

Finally, after the impish woman who seemed to bat her eyes at the duke every other minute was gone, Eva let out the breath she had been holding all night. As she turned wearily to head up the stairs to her own room, however, she was stopped by the clammy hand that grasped her wrist.

"I would like for you to stay a moment, my harp."

Eva bristled. "I've told you I hate that name."

"Nevertheless, I need for you to stay."

"As if I have any choice," Eva grumbled, walking back down the steps. She followed him back to the dining room, nearly getting hit in the face by the door when he let it fall shut behind him.

To her relief, Jack was still in the room, helping one of the servants pick up a tray of dishes that seemed to have been dropped. But the moment their eyes met, the duke cleared his throat.

"I would like everyone else to leave. My beloved—"

Eva stopped dead in her tracks. "I am *not* your beloved."

"Eva," he said in a patient tone, "I would appreciate you not speaking to me in that tone in my own house, my harp."

Eva stared at him. He couldn't be serious. "I am going to say this very slowly and very carefully," she said. "I. Am not. Your blooming harp!"

He turned back and closed the distance between them. "Eva," he said in a soft voice, "I love you. I wish you would understand that. I apologize if I have not made this clear before, but I do love you!"

"And how in the continent would you know that?" She stomped over to the large windows. "I don't think you would know real love if it bit you on the—"

"I've read so many times," he held up his hands and looked at them, "that when your palms get sweaty, you must be in love! In the poetry . . . I would not have written that had it not been for my obvious admiration for you, despite some of your physical short-comings."

"That!" Eva threw up her hands. "*That* is exactly the kind of thing one does not say if one is in love!"

The duke straightened and tugged on his jacket. "And how would you know what love is or isn't? It's not as though you've ever taken enough of a chance to know about love. In fact, that's one of the reasons I decided to love you. You never take risks."

That stung more than Eva wanted to admit, but she ground her teeth and did her best to make sure he couldn't see her pain. "I may not have boys trailing behind me or lining up for my hand on the dance floor, but I know for certain what love *isn't*. And it isn't kidnapping. And it isn't threatening someone's family. And it most *definitely* is not having sweaty palms." Eva shuddered. "That's just repugnant." She crossed her arms in case he decided to take her hand again.

Instead of trying to take her hand, the duke reached into his coat and pulled out a folded piece of parchment. He handed it to Eva and clasped his hands behind his back.

"If you read it, you will see that I have not threatened your family in any way." His eyes brightened a little. "See? Love."

For one brief moment, Eva considered crumpling the parchment up and throwing it into the fireplace behind her. Instead, she untied the ribbon and unfolded the parchment. As she began to read, her heart dropped into her stomach, and by the time she was halfway through, her determination to not allow him any emotion crumbled. She gasped and threw a hand over her mouth.

"I know about your cupbearer," he said softly.

Eva could only continue to read the awful parchment in horror.

"But I'm willing to forgive you for your infidelity once you sign this and Jack is gone. Then we begin anew, and our love will blossom the way it was always meant to."

"Infidelity?" Her head was suddenly too fuzzy to make sense of the words. "Gone?"

"He must be gone by morning." The duke looked at her patiently. "Now, now, you didn't think I wouldn't notice that you two have become somewhat of an odd little couple lately. Or that I was ignorant of his designs?" He chuckled. "He was far too covered in magic residue that first day to have been any sort of servant. Besides, he really is a terrible servant."

"Then why did you allow him to stay?" Eva asked, unable to help herself.

The duke shrugged. "As long as he was here, you weren't going anywhere." He pulled a pen from his sleeve. "Now all you need to do is sign."

Eva ran a few steps back and held the parchment over the fire just out of reach of the hungry flames. "I'm not signing this."

"I would be careful with that. The contract has been spelled, and burning it would only bring its threats to pass."

Eva yanked the paper back and clutched it to her chest.

"As to the question about signing it, I could simply kill him now."

Eva's knees threatened to buckle as the duke came forward and took her hands in his sweaty ones.

"But really, consider his sendoff a gift. If I didn't care about your feelings, immoral as they may be, I would have had him killed upon arrival."

Eva closed her eyes and took a deep breath, counting until she was in less danger of saying something she regretted that might endanger Jack more. When she was finally able to speak again, she did so in slow, measured tones.

"What is this about my having to wed on that particular day? That doesn't even make sense."

The duke wagged his finger and gave her a knowing smile. "You may be ignorant in a number of ways, dear harp, but I know enough of your tricks now to know that if you could change our wedding day, you would, and you would do nearly anything to delay it. So if you are not married on *that* particular day listed, which is precisely a week from today, someone somewhere will die." He shrugged. "I'm not entirely sure who it would be. The king will be present at the wedding, as will every noble in the land. And lots of commoners, for good will, of course."

"You filthy—"

"Let's not speak that way to one another now." He put a finger on her lips. "Look, I'll even have a horse and carriage prepared to take Jim—"

"Jack."

"That's what I said. Jake and his family to another place. Astoria, if you would like! But you must convince him to leave, or there's little else I can do." The duke held the pen out again. "It really is better for everyone this way. Jake will escape the farm life he never wanted, and you'll be queen!"

Eva couldn't bring herself to respond as she slowly took the pen. Her hand shook as she placed it against the table. Desperately, silently, she racked her brain for any other way. But the more she thought, the more she realized there was none. The scratch of the pen hurt her ears as she signed her name and watched her dreams depart.

"I'll give you the night to convince him to go," the duke called out after her as she fled up the stairs, "but by supper tomorrow, he must be gone."

14

NO, BUT YOU WILL

*E*va trudged back to her room. How was she supposed to tell Jack that he had to leave if she couldn't tell him the reason why?

She hadn't realized just how much she had come to rely on him. Whenever the duke insulted her, the insults didn't hurt quite as much as they had at first because she knew Jack would be there when the duke left to tell her the cruel words weren't true. She had remembered how to smile, even on her long, tortuous walks with her captor, because Jack was always a few steps behind, ready to share an amused glance at whatever bizarre attempt at wooing the duke was determined to try next. Jack thought she was brave. He thought she was beautiful.

And now, she was going to have to break him.

Perhaps, she thought as she walked into her room and shut the door, she could come up with some other way to get him to leave. Perhaps she should remind him of how much his brothers would need him by now. After all, Mortimer wasn't exactly the most reliable babysitter, particularly if Jack's mother showed as little interest in her children as Jack made it sound. And though the duke had made it clear Jack wouldn't be able to share what he knew, perhaps she could inadvertently send some sort of message to her cousin to send to her family. They must be worried sick by now. She could only imagine Rynn, Sophie, and Martin setting off to find her, insisting that the younger girls (which Martin would insist his twin was, despite being his twin) needed to stay home.

And if it were up to her siblings, they just might find a way to pull off a rescue. Maybe.

Just maybe.

Her spirits rose a little as she sat down at her harp to play the evening song. It wasn't difficult to dredge up feelings of sorrow for the song itself, but when she was finished, she was able to sit down at her desk to write her letter without total panic taking control of her.

"Eva!" a hissed whisper sounded.

Eva looked around. But there was no one to be seen. Just an empty room.

"Eva! The balcony!" the shouted whisper came again.

Slowly, Eva rose. "Which balcony?"

There was a pause. "The one on the side of the mountain."

She followed the voice to the western balcony that faced the mountain. When she stepped outside, she stopped and looked around.

"Psst! Behind you!"

Eva turned to see Jack perched up on the roof. Spread out around him were little bowls of food, as well as teacups, utensils, empty plates, and two goblets.

"I thought in celebration of surviving the night, as well as finding out where he keeps his beloved Golden Goose ledger, we might as well celebrate."

Eva's heart twisted as he hopped down and held out his hands. Without thinking, she put hers in them, and he twirled her around into a position where they could dance. And as they began swaying from side to side in a slow circle, she closed her eyes and wished with all her heart that this duty hadn't fallen to her.

"You've never had a suitor before, correct?" Jack asked as they danced. "A serious one, I mean."

She could only stare at him miserably and shake her head.

He nodded sharply. "That's what I thought. So this should be educational for you as well as celebratory."

Curiosity got the better of her. "Why would that be?" she asked.

"Because you need to know how a real man woos a woman."

"A real man?" She couldn't contain her smile completely.

"What the duke is trying to do is absolutely not what you should expect from a real man." He gently took one of her hands and held it up. "For demonstration purposes only."

Eva couldn't help laughing at his solemn expression. "Of course."

"When a gentleman wishes to seek your hand, he should do so with flowers or long evening walks . . . properly escorted, of course. Or even with cookies. Kidnapping, however," he held up a finger and wagged it at her, "is strictly prohibited. Any such fop who attempts to gain your affections in such a manner should be promptly thumped on the head and handed over to the authorities. Not courted." He raised his eyebrows. "Are you paying attention?"

Eva nodded, smiling in spite of herself.

He nodded once to himself and then gestured up to the roof. "And when the courtship proceeds to the point where it is appropriate to have a meal together, again properly chaperoned, it is important to remember that no fellow worth noticing will give you food that makes your mouth itch. And he most definitely will not make you eat it. Still following?"

Unable to bring herself to the dreaded conversation she knew was coming, Eva decided to play along, even if it meant just a few more moments of fun and then a heartbreak worse than ever to follow.

"And what should I do if he asks me to dance?" She put her hands on her hips and raised an eyebrow at him.

"I'm glad you asked." He took her hands in his again and placed one of them on his shoulder and the other on his arm. She couldn't help noticing the calluses on his hands that were absent from the duke's hands, or the sturdiness of his shoulders beneath the servant's uniform.

"When he asks you to dance, and only if he *asks* you to dance, again as kidnapping should never be tolerated—"

"Shhh!" Eva laughed softly as she glanced over the edge of the balcony. "Someone might hear you!"

"No interruptions, please. Now, as I was saying, if someone asks you to dance, you may either accept their offer," his hands tightened infinitesimally on her waist and fingers, "or you may refuse them and call them whatever sort of names you wish."

"What if I don't want to call them names?"

"Then there is the chance," his voice softened and the dancing slowed just slightly, "that he might come under the impression that you don't completely despise him."

Eva's voice caught in her throat. "Would that be so awful?" she asked breathlessly.

He leaned down even more until his forehead was touching hers, and she could feel the heat from his breath on her lips. "Not if that's what you really wanted."

As he began to close the distance, however, a light behind him flickered. Eva's heart stopped. That was the duke's window. And she was going to get Jack killed if she wasn't careful.

"I think . . . I think you need to go," she whispered, wanting to kick herself as she uttered the words.

He froze. She could feel him tense up then he slowly let go of her and took a step back.

"I'm sorry," he said, looking down at the ground. "I . . . I just thought—"

"I'm going to marry the duke, and there's nothing we can do about it." She forced her voice to sound cold. "So we might as well not hurt ourselves even more within necessity."

"Wait a minute, now." He took a step closer again. "Where is this coming from? A few hours ago, you and I were planning your escape." She could see him frown even in the dim light of the new moon. "Why are you suddenly the pessimist?"

She turned and took a few steps away so he couldn't see her cry. "Tonight . . . tonight proved that we won't win. We can't. You saw him in there. He even has the rest of the nobility at his fingertips! And most of them hate him! How can we hope to beat that?" She dug her fingernails into her palms to keep the trembling from her voice. "Besides, Mortimer is hardly the best babysitter. And if your mother is as negligent as you make her seem, it will be a miracle if your brothers have survived this long. It would be best if you took them and left Guthward."

There was a long silence. But instead of leaving, he marched up behind her and whirled her around. When she came to face him again, his jaw was tight, and his eyes burned with the light of the candles he'd lit on the ledge behind her.

"I don't know what he told you or what you're trying to do here, but it's not going to work. I'm not leaving you! Especially not with that madman—"

"You talk about staying with me, but in the end, you'll have to go. Sometime, you will have to quit."

"No, I won't!"

"Yes! You will!" But even as she said the words, Eva knew he wasn't going to budge. So she took a deep breath and tried again. "In one week, I am marrying the duke. Soon after, he will be king and I will be queen, and there is nothing you or I or anyone else can do about it."

"I am not going to leave you!"

Why was he making this so incredibly hard? Eva looked into his eyes and put as much venom in her words as she could muster. "What did you think could come of this? Even if there was anything between us, what then?"

"Eva, I—"

"I'll go back to my family, and you'll go back to your mother.

And when you ask her permission to come and court me, she'll say no because she won't want you to live a better life than her. And you'll fight and quarrel, but in the end, you'll remain with her and do her bidding, because that's what you always do. I'll be stuck, waiting, and you'll never come because you always listen to Mother! And you'll always be a quitter because you've never learned to be a man, and because you're a quitter, you'll never learn to stand on your own—"

"Stop. Just stop."

Eva hated herself as the pain crossed his face in a shadow she wished she could erase. But she had purposefully chosen the very words that would leave a scar, even if time healed them, and his last memory of her would be the one where she made his heart bleed.

The silence was so thick Eva thought it just might suffocate her. When he finally lifted his eyes from the ground and met hers once more, his words were almost inaudible. But the raw pain within them hurt like nothing she'd ever felt before. Not even the duke's most cutting insults could compare.

"If that's really what you think of me." He slowly turned to walk back to the wall that she assumed he had used to climb up to her balcony. He put his hands against the railing and leaned over, but paused there. "And you're determined to do this?"

"I am."

He nodded but said nothing else. Eva wanted nothing more than to run to him and take it all back. She longed to throw her arms around his neck and beg for forgiveness. Only the memory of the threats on the parchment kept her rooted to her spot.

"You say you want to live," he said after a long moment. "But you should know that you'll never live if you don't learn to fight." And with that, he was gone.

"No," Eva whispered, tears rolling down her face as she hugged herself and sank down to the ground. "But you will."

15

YOU'RE MUCH MORE VIOLENT THAN I WOULD HAVE EXPECTED

"Try not to look so sad, my dear," Mrs. McConnell said as she fluffed Eva's veil once more. "You really do look lovely. Besides, this is only a fitting. You have several days more." When Eva didn't respond, she paused in her work and looked up. "Eva . . ."

"My mother always spoke of my wedding day," Eva said as she stared into the mirror.

"Most mothers do. Any mother worth the title, at least."

But Eva shook her head. "There were six of us girls. More than enough wedding days to go around." She sighed. "But she always said she couldn't wait to see me in my gown. She said . . ." Her voice hitched.

"She said what, dear?" Mrs. McConnell put a hand on Eva's lace-covered shoulder.

Eva couldn't manage more than a whisper. "She wanted to see my eyes shine for a boy the way they did for my music. Because then she knew I would be truly happy."

Mrs. McConnell's own eyes grew a little glassy after that. It was just the pollen in the air, she swore. It made her eyes water. But not much more was said until Eva's gown was fitted and removed, and Eva had returned to her usual green.

"Don't forget," the housekeeper said quietly as she gathered up her sewing supplies, "you have a walk with the master in an hour." Then she left Eva alone.

Eva tried to return to bed to rest. She hadn't slept well in the days since Jack had left and didn't come back. This should have comforted her, she chided herself again and again. After all, that was what she wanted, wasn't it? If he had stayed, the duke would have had him executed on the spot. Or perhaps he would have used some horrid magic trick to make the death more interesting. Eva shivered.

And yet, she couldn't remember the last time she'd felt so alone. Before Jack had arrived, Eva hadn't expected anything else. She was alone, and she knew it. But now she expected to see his face every time she turned around. Whenever she trailed behind the duke on their walks, she would find herself glancing over her shoulder in search of a pair of slate-gray eyes that followed her every move. The duke's cutting remarks about her ignorance or imperfections weren't funny anymore, as there was no one there to remind her of their foolishness.

But Jack was safe, and that's what was important. As Eva lay there, however, unable to even keep her eyes shut for fear of seeing his face whenever she did, a new fire burned in her belly. Everything here was wrong. They had spent so much time scheming and planning, and the duke had still managed to ruin it all in a single swoop. One man shouldn't have the power to make everyone around him cower in fear, magic or no magic. He shouldn't get a bride because he felt like taking one. And Jack was ten times the man the duke could ever be. A hundred times. Why should the duke have the ability to yank everyone about like puppets on a string?

No matter how Eva looked at it, the trail of fault led back to one person.

Eva leapt to her feet and rolled her sleeves up.

"Oh detestable godfather Mortimer, I, your kidnapped goddaughter, demand you come and face the consequences for what you've done."

Nothing happened.

"Mortimer, I know you're there. You're required to come when I summon you, and I've summoned you."

"You didn't do it right," a familiar voice whined. No body appeared, but Eva knew she had him.

"I'm not going to say it."

"It's, 'Oh great fairy godfather Mortimer, I, a stupid human, humbly need your magnificent and wonderful magic.' Now try again."

"No." Eva stomped her foot. "I will not try again. And I will say nothing of the sort. Now you get your sorry rump here and listen for once in your life!"

The contours of a man's form began to take shape beside the fireplace. As his shadow thickened, the scents of body odor and sawdust began to grow stronger as well. The gray robe, which was far too large, covered all but his scruffy, unshaven face.

Eva wrinkled her nose. "How long has it been since you've had a bath?"

"Someone's sensitive today!" He shook off his hood and grimaced. "And I always liked you best."

"Because I never called on you."

"Precisely."

"Did you ever stop and wonder why that was?" Eva crossed her arms. "Did it ever occur to you that there was a purpose behind that?"

Mortimer looked at her as though she'd spoken gibberish. "It wasn't just because you were content?"

"No! It was because I felt sorry for you!"

Mortimer's face went blank. "Sorry for me?"

"Yes!" Eva threw her hands up. "Because I know what it's like to have a passion! I had my harp, and you had your experiments, and I never thought it was fair of the fairy council to require you to grant wishes if you didn't want to!"

"Oh."

"But those days are long over!"

"Oh?" Mortimer looked around. "Where's that fellow I sent after you?"

"I had to send him home."

"Well, that was your—"

"To keep him safe!"

The fairy held up a finger and closed his eyes. After a moment, he opened them again. "I think you may need to go back and explain this in a little more detail."

Eva stomped over to her bed, picked up a pillow, and threw it at him as hard as she could. "I can't!"

"Why not? Hey, stop that!"

Eva threw another pillow, ignoring the fairy's protests. "Because I can't! I wish I could, but I *can't*. I. Can't." She glared at him, willing him to understand.

He stared at her blankly for a long time. But eventually, understanding began to dawn on his face.

"Oh. So you can't tell me why—"

"No."

"Not even who—"

"What part of *no* do you not understand, Mortimer?"

He frowned at her. "Then why did you summon me?"

"Because you need to understand what happens when you use magic so carelessly!" Eva exploded. "You are the reason I was kidnapped because you were the one that cursed me with this infernal gift!"

He scratched his grizzly chin. "And just why is it my fault?"

Eva seriously considered screaming. Was he really that dense? "When you publicly gifted me the ability to grow or kill plants with my harp, the duke heard about it. He chased me until he found me hiding with my cousin for this very reason. And when he kidnapped me, and you sent Jack, you put Jack's life in danger as well. And now I'm going to marry the duke and Jack is in danger, and it's all your fault!"

Mortimer rolled his sleeves up as he paced back and forth in front of her fireplace. After a long silence, he finally looked at her again.

"So . . . you don't want to marry the duke?"

Eva threw another pillow. "What do you think?"

"You can stop that now! You're angry. I'm aware. No need to be so mean." He paused. "If you didn't want it, why didn't you just ask me not to give you the gift in the first place?"

"I did! But apparently, the only way to get you to listen is to throw things at you!"

"You're much more violent than I would have expected. I always thought you were the nice one."

"You're still not listening to me!" Eva cried, a little louder than she meant to. Against her will, tears began to fall, and her voice broke into a choked sob. "When you gave me this magic without even considering what I thought of it, you forced me into a life of this!" She spread her arms out.

Mortimer looked around. "It's a pretty extravagant room, if you ask me."

"Extravagant, yes! But it comes with daily reminders from the one person who *should* love me most that I'm not pretty enough, or that I'm a country bumpkin, or that I will never, ever be good enough for the man I marry! And I will live with those reminders until the day I die."

Mortimer was silent as he stared at the ground. Finally, he lifted his head and looked at her. And though Eva had seen him dozens of time over the course of her life, she realized it was the first time he'd probably ever really *seen* her. When he spoke again, his voice was finally rid of its general sarcasm.

"What do you need? Really?"

She held his gaze and crossed her arms. "I need you to promise to keep my family and Jack's family safe from the duke and all those under his influence."

He nodded, but she held up a finger.

"And no rodents. Or anything that's rabid."

He began to scowl. "You can't tell me how I'm going to—"

"You owe me, Mortimer."

He held her glare for a long moment before shrugging and giving a huff. "Very well. What next?"

"Take away my gift."

"Can't do that."

"What?" she cried.

"Sorry. I can't just take away a gift after I give it."

"Meaning you don't know how."

"Does it make a difference?" he snapped.

She rolled her eyes. Then she walked to the balcony that faced the mountain. She needed to think. She could ask him to spell her husband-to-be, but then she thought better of it. Fairy godparents couldn't kill, and with Mortimer's skill set, the duke would probably see it coming. It was the whole reason she hadn't summoned him sooner. He would just make an even bigger mess of things. So she would have to be the one to beat the duke. The hopes of all of Guthward couldn't hinge on Mortimer. *She* would have to be tricky. She would have to—

Eva stopped as the gleam of her harp caught her eye. She stepped closer and fingered the instrument, running her hand down its smooth golden curve. A ferocious desire began to claw its way out of her stomach and into her head.

"What else?" Mortimer called from her room.

Eva smiled. "I'm not going to go quietly." She thought of Jack and smiled even more. "For once, I'm not going to play it safe. I'm going to *live*."

16

YOU REALLY ARE A TERRIBLE FAIRY

*J*ack tugged on the collar of his shirt for the thousandth time since he'd started walking, but it was no use. Though he was in his old clothes and no longer in the ridiculous green uniform, the humidity was stifling, even for Guthward. Just breathing was like trying to drink the air. Of course, it didn't help that his mood was already far sourer than the water in a stagnant pond.

Where had they gone wrong?

It was the question he'd asked himself over and over again since Eva had practically thrown him out the night before. And as he'd stolen his horse back from the duke's stables where he'd hidden him, then followed the hidden green path home by the light of the moon, Jack hadn't been able to come up with an answer.

He was fairly confident that the duke had threatened Eva. It was the only explanation he could come up with that satisfied the confusion that threatened to turn his gut inside out.

They'd been laughing and talking together only that morning. Even up until she'd had to leave him to be escorted by the duke to that awful dinner party, he had dared to hope that she might have feelings for him . . . something deeper than a general sense of gratitude for his help. The way she'd watched him whenever they were near, the look in her eyes that made him feel as though she were a ship at sea and he was her anchor. She hadn't hesitated to reach out to him whenever she needed his assistance. She'd even nudged him with her shoulder the day before as they'd shared a joke at the duke's expense right behind his back. It hadn't been intimate by any romantic standards, but the touch had felt so . . . well, so natural. It had felt right. They'd only known one another for a month, and yet, he felt strange trying to imagine life without her.

And then, there on the balcony as they'd danced, he'd been so close to giving in to the ever-growing urge that had been present for weeks now. It would have been so easy to close the last few inches between their lips. He could almost feel her mouth against his, despite never having kissed a girl in his life.

Well, a real kiss. That peck back in the study hadn't been nearly long enough.

And then, without explanation, she was done. Giving up. Accepting what the duke had laid out for her, and she hadn't been willing to even consider his position.

Well, fine then! She could stay there with that poor excuse for a man, and he would go on his merry way. He would get his family and head for the nearest place that wasn't Guthward. In theory.

Unfortunately, his head and his heart couldn't come to a full understanding.

Jack for the entire night along his magic green path, grumbling even more to himself when he realized all the plants aside from his strange path were still dead. He must have left the duke's lands, which meant he wouldn't find a breakfast of berries or even be able to chew on dandelions along the way.

By the time he arrived home the next morning, he was not in a good mood.

"Jack!" Ray spotted him first and came running out of the barn to greet him, with Larry close on his heels. Jack's heart softened a little when they threw their arms around his waist. "We missed you!"

"Some strange man came and said he'd sent you on a quest," Larry said. "He also said he was a fairy, but I didn't believe him."

"But then I asked him to prove it, and he did!" Ray jumped up and down.

Jack frowned down at his little brother. "How did he do that?"

"We asked him to make us new toys."

"And what toys did he make you?" Jack asked.

Ray sprinted back to the barn, disappeared for a moment, then came sprinting back. As he grew closer, Jack could see that he was holding a miniature axe.

"Larry has one, too! But his is smaller than mine. Then the fairy said we should have races to see who could run fastest while carrying them!"

The fairy had given them axes to play with. Axes. Of all the stupid . . . Jack took a deep calming breath. "You don't run with an axe, you ninnies. Where is Mother?"

"She's in the house," Ray said, rolling his eyes. "As usual."

"Did she help you at all while I was gone?" Jack shook his head. "Never mind. Don't answer that. Look, I want both of you to get a bag and fill it with the things you like most. We're leaving."

The boys' eyes grew wide.

"Leaving?" Larry said in a quiet voice.

"Where are we going?" Ray asked. "And for how long?"

"Just do as you're told. I'll tell you more later, but we have to go soon." He strode toward the house, but then he paused. "And no matter what you hear Mother say, I want you to keep preparing. And hook the horses to the cart when you're done. They need to be ready to go by the time I get back."

Whether it was his tone or their desire to be far away when he talked to their mother, Jack didn't know, but the boys ran off without hesitation. Jack squared his shoulders and resumed his walk to the house. Now came the hard part.

"Mother!" he called as he walked inside. "Mother, I'm back. And we need to go. Now."

His mother appeared in the doorway to her room. From the frizz of her hair and the scowl on her face, she looked to have been in bed.

"What's all this fuss about? You go away and leave us on our own for weeks, and then you jig your way back in here and expect us to up and leave?" She took another step closer. "And since when are you giving orders around here?"

"Since I've been to a very bad place, and I'm fairly certain the bad man from the bad place will be coming to get me at any time." Jack knew better than to try and tell her the details of his situation. He'd tried with no less than three travelers he'd met on the way home, begging them to help him contact the king. But every time he'd opened his mouth to recount his tale, garbled nonsense came out. It was maddening. So the best he could give were ambiguous statements.

"Pshaw." She waved a hand and turned back into her room. "You can go then. But the boys and I are staying here."

He followed her into her room, where he found her getting back into bed. "Are you sick?"

"There's no reason to get out of bed if the crops won't grow."

"We still have animals to feed! And you've left the boys to do *everything* on their own?"

"They're big enough. A mother deserves a day to rest now and then."

Jack stomped over to her little window and peeked out. Every second, he expected to hear the clatter of a carriage or the clip-clop of guard horses. The duke had never said as much, but he had made his superiority quite clear. It was only a matter of time before he came to prove once and for all that he had power over Jack. And with his failure to bring Eva back, Jack was rather sure the fairy's protection was now expired as well.

When he was sure that the yard was still clear, he hurried over to the single wooden dresser in the far corner of the room and began to pull clothes out, stuffing them into the nearest bag he could find.

"What are you doing?" His mother shot up in bed once more.

"I told you, bad people are coming. And they're not going to care if I'm gone. When they find out this is where I lived, they're going to take you and the boys and hurt you."

"Stop that!" She got out of bed and tried to yank the bag away. "We're not going anywhere! Not with you, at least."

"You've always wanted to leave. This is your chance!"

She pulled harder. "Not like this! Running for our lives like common thieves!"

Jack paused and stared hard at his mother. Her graying red hair stuck out in wisps all over her head, and her eyes were bright with indignation.

She had once been pretty, he recalled. Before his father died, back when she laughed, and there were hugs and sometimes even kind words, she had been pretty. But now she glowered at him with those piercing eyes, and the joy that had once occasionally appeared on her face was gone. Her clothes were frayed, as though she no longer saw any need to patch them, and her hair looked as though she hadn't bothered to comb it.

Hopeless. She looked hopeless.

"Mother," he whispered. "I want to keep you safe. I'm trying in the best way I know how. But I don't know what else to do." He held his hands out helplessly, letting the bag drop. "I know you blame me for Father's death. And I'm sorry. If I could go back and change things, I would have. But hating me isn't going to help the boys, and it's not going to help you. Please," he took a step closer, willing her to keep eye contact with him, to see his earnestness and remember that she had once loved him, too. "Let me keep us safe. Let me do what Father would have wanted done."

She studied him for a long time, and for a moment, he thought her expression might have softened. But then her mouth set in a harder line than before, and she turned her back on him and climbed back in bed.

"You can peddle your dreams somewhere else, Jack, but you don't fool me. Your father gave up on us. And you're no better than him. We aren't going anywhere. At least not with you."

"But you've always wanted to leave . . ." He put his hands on his face and rubbed his eyes. "Look. I didn't do what I set out to do, so my deal with the fairy is done."

She didn't seem surprised by his mention of a fairy. The boys must have told her. Or perhaps Mortimer had visited her himself. Either way, she didn't seem to think it necessary to mention. Instead, she donned a pinched, sour expression. "That's a surprise."

"That means the food will stop. The protection will stop. So if the boys get hurt, or worse, because you won't let them leave? What happens then?"

She drew her legs up to her chin and glared at the little fireplace ahead of her. "I am the leader of this family. What I say goes." She sniffed. "So if you want to continue being a part of it, I suggest you stop with all this nonsense."

Jack folded his arms across his chest. "Then I'll take the boys and go."

"I'll call the constable and report you for kidnapping."

Jack whirled around and stomped out, slamming the door behind him. As he continued out into the yard, Ray called out from the barn.

"We've got the cart and horses ready to go!"

Jack ignored his brother and continued marching on toward the pigpen.

"Jack?" Larry shouted. "Aren't we going?"

"I don't know!" Jack bellowed back. When he finally got to the pen, he climbed up on the fence and glared down at the mud below.

Eva had been right. As much as her words stung, he was a coward. And even worse, his mother had been right, too. He was a quitter. He had gone on a quest and not only failed to bring back the girl he'd set out to save in the first place, but he was now letting his mother control him. Again.

Well, no more. Jack was done quitting. And he was done letting his mother control his life. From now on, he was going to make his own choices. He was going back to the duke's mansion, and he was going to bring Eva back, even if he had to drag her out kicking and screaming.

Of course, he needed to do something with the boys first. And then he had to figure out exactly *how* he was going to get Eva away from the duke, particularly if it was going to be against her will.

"She was always my favorite, you know."

Jack jumped at the voice behind him. When he saw who it was, however, his mood only grew dourer.

The fairy stood behind him. Unlike the first time they'd met, however, his tiny wings were drooped, and he looked cowed, staring at the ground. As he spoke, he picked at a hole in his robe.

"I never liked any of them much. But of all the children in the woodcutter's family, I never resented her quite like the others."

Jack really wanted to tell the fairy what he could do with his likes and dislikes, but he also wanted to know more about Eva.

"So, what was it that convinced you not to dislike her?"

The fairy sighed as though the confession pained him. "She let me be. The other children all got curious at some point in time, and every time I showed up, they had questions. 'Could you make me taller?' 'Why did you make Mummy and Daddy merchants?' 'How does Sophie always know what time it is?' 'Why did you make me beautiful? Boys aren't supposed to be beautiful.'" Mortimer made a gagging sound. "They were all either ungrateful or greedy. Eva was the only one that let me be completely."

"So you cursed her with magic when she asked you not to," Jack said, nodding. "That makes perfect sense."

"Look, I've had to endure abuse from her entire family." He shuddered so hard his cloak quivered. "Particularly the middle brat . . . the wicked one. I don't need it from you, too."

"Then why are you here?"

"I want to know why you left," Mortimer said.

"I would tell you," Jack crossed his arms over his chest, "but it seems I'm not allowed to talk about it. More lovely magic, I'm sure."

"Oh." Mortimer fumbled with his sleeves and then slapped Jack across the face.

"Ow! What was that for?"

"I'm removing the spell of silence the duke placed on you."

"I thought you couldn't intrude on another fairy's magic."

"The problem is that I'm not supposed to interfere with my own magic once it's been cast."

"Won't?" Jack raised an eyebrow. "Or can't?"

"Does it really matter?"

Jack shrugged and grinned. "No. It just proves beyond a doubt that you truly are an awful fairy."

Mortimer scowled. "Look! My point is that I can lift the duke's spell of silence on you because he used *purchased* magic. Magic is much less potent when inside an object vessel rather than a human. And even less so when that object has been bought rather than gifted directly from a fairy. And, on top of that, you aren't the main target of the spell. You're sort of an afterthought. I don't have to break the spell, just cut you off from it. It makes it a good deal easier. Here though, for good measure." He smacked Jack across the other cheek.

"Do you have to do it so hard?" Jack rubbed his head.

"No," the fairy said with a smug smile. Then he pulled the left side of his cloak open and searched it for a moment before giving up and searching on the right. Jack rolled his eyes as the fairy then pulled off a shoe and peered inside.

Before Jack could make another sarcastic remark, however, Mortimer snapped his fingers and reached low to the bottom of his cloak. From a hidden spot Jack couldn't see, Mortimer produced a rolled parchment tied with a string.

"Do you want to know why she chased you away?" He held the parchment out.

Jack took the paper, unrolled it, and began to read.

In signing this contract, Eva, daughter of the fairy-blessed woodcutter family housed in Astoria, agrees to the following:

First, she agrees to engage in matrimony to the duke of Monte David on the first day of this eighth month of the year as dated above. If she fails to be married by midnight of the aforementioned date, another person who shall be chosen at random will die at the stroke of midnight.

Second, if any other being is made aware of or discovers this contract, Jack, who assumed the role of cupbearer for Eva during the summer months, shall die at the stroke of midnight as well.

And there at the bottom of the page in neat, small handwriting was Eva's name.

"How did you get this?" Jack asked.

"After Eva summoned me to yell at me, I went poking around the duke's study." He smirked. "Not bad, eh?"

Jack had to read the letter three times before he was able to comprehend the whole of it. But with each reading, relief covered him like dew of the morning. So she hadn't betrayed him. She'd been trying to save his life.

"I should have seen this coming," he muttered as he read the letter yet again.

"But you didn't. So here we are."

"You can't act all high and mighty there, either." Jack said, not looking up at the fairy. "If the duke had gotten all his wording right for the magic, I would have been dead by now."

"What? Let me see that?" Mortimer snatched the contract up and read it for himself. "Huh," he said several times before looking back down at Jack. "Well isn't that something?"

"How are you a fairy godfather?" Jack asked, exasperated. "My death wouldn't be a concern for your superiors?"

"Oh, it would have been . . . in an eon or so. Whenever the fairy council decided to convene again." Mortimer shrugged. "I was just trying to help. Wait, what are you doing?"

Jack had turned and headed for the barn. Mortimer followed him, still clutching the parchment. Inside the barn Jack began to unharness one of the horses from the cart.

"While I'm gone," he said as he worked, "I need you to take my brothers to Eva's house in Astoria. Make sure they get there safely." He paused and glared at the fairy. "And in their human form. Not in the shape of a rodent or bird or whatever suits your fancy."

Mortimer spat on the ground. "I'm not your godfather. You can't tell me what to do."

"I can when I'm trying to save *your* goddaughter. Now listen closely. After my brothers are safe, I need you to tell her family what's happened and where we are."

"Or where she is, since you'll likely be dead," Mortimer muttered under his breath.

Jack laughed as he mounted his horse. "You really are a terrible fairy, aren't you?"

Mortimer muttered something about respect and the possibility of finding spiders in one's bed.

"The beanstalk is still there, isn't it?" Jack asked.

"Yes, unfortunately." Mortimer crossed his arms. "So you're just running back to the home of the man who wants to kill you. What exactly do you plan to do when you get there?"

Jack grinned. "I'm going to steal the duke's harp."

17

I WOULD LIKE TO HONOR HIM WITH
A SONG

"Mary," Eva called as she walked into the kitchen, "has the duke given you a list of the dishes he's chosen for the wedding?"

"Yes'm," the girl replied, tucking a stray lock of strawberry hair behind her ear. She untied her apron and hung it on a hook by the door before beckoning Eva to the little nook in the corner. On their way over, Eva had to dodge several enthusiastic little boys who had been tasked with running food to certain parts of the kitchen.

"You certainly stay busy down here," she remarked as Mary opened a box and began thumbing through a stack of parchments.

"Yes,'m. Although we're not always like this. It's the wedding and all." She removed the quill tucked behind her ear and used it to point at the scribblings on the parchment she'd pulled out of the stack. "Bert's working on the meat. Darcy has the produce, and Mister Matt's got the sweets. You've never lived until you've tried one of Mister Matt's cherry tarts."

"Then that's exactly what I shall do." Eva smiled at the girl. "Did you find the menu?"

"Here you go." Mary handed her a parchment. Then she blushed a little, making the sprinkling of freckles on her nose and cheeks stand out against her pale skin. "I hope you don't mind me saying so," she said shyly, "but the staff's right happy you're staying here. You . . ." Her eyes widened and she looked down. "We're happy you're here."

"What were you going to say?" Eva tried to meet the girl's bright blue eyes once more. "You needn't fear anything from me. I promise."

Mary studied her for a moment longer, though, before adding quietly, "You . . . you soften things around here. When you're around, no one's as worried." She shrugged. "It's nice."

"Even when I throw fits?" Eva felt guilty as she remembered the monumental tantrum she'd had the day before when the duke had tried to get her to try beet juice. Unfortunately, since Jack had arrived, her fits had worked less and less. And now that he was gone, the duke hardly listened to her at all.

"Aw, we know those are for the master." Mary glanced over her shoulder before leaning closer. "We're not supposed to know why you're here. But we do. And we understand why it's hard for you."

"Tell me," Eva tucked the menu under her arm and turned her back to the kitchen so no one else could see her face, "why did you get a job with the duke? Out here we're far from any other residences, and he isn't exactly a . . . soft master, as you put it."

Mary began restacking the other parchments she'd gone through to find the menu. "My mum's rather sickly. And working here may not be easy, but it pays good, and we needed the coin. And now we have food better than anyone else in Guthward." She stopped and eyed Eva once more. "You won't tell the master?"

Eva shook her head quickly. "Oh, no! I was just curious." She gave Mary a wry smile. "If you hadn't noticed, I didn't exactly come here on my own accord."

After parting ways, Eva grabbed an apple from where one of the servant girls was chopping fruit for pies, then she seated herself on one of the little balcony seats just beneath the duke's study window, placing a bottle of ink beside her. Every few moments, as she marked up the menu with a quill, she would glance up. She was prepared to wait for several hours, as the duke had been quite busy that morning, but only ten minutes had passed before he spotted her and made his way down to where she was seated.

"What are you doing, my harp?" He eyed the parchment in her hand, and a grin slowly began to spread across his face. "Would those be wedding details you're seeing to?"

Eva gave a loud sigh. "I've been thinking, and I suppose as this wedding party really *is* to take place, I would benefit more if I contributed as well, just as any bride would."

The duke took the parchment and looked at it. He nodded slowly as he read her notes. Finally, he handed it back.

"While I'm not partial to all these changes, I suppose the change in your attitude is worth it. Yes, my harp, you may make all the changes to the menu that you wish." He beamed and puffed his chest out. "I'm so glad you've come around. I always knew you would. A good girl like you couldn't go on fighting the inevitable forever, particularly as it benefits you so."

"My lord." A few men walked up and bowed to the duke. "Might we have a word about one of the storehouses? The last storm left its roof rather weak."

"Of course. Well, you'll have to excuse me, my harp." The duke patted Eva's cheek before heading off with the men. Eva didn't move until he was out of sight, then she scrambled back inside. It was hard not to smile to herself as she searched for the house-keeper. The duke had seemed to believe her story. Now the real fun could begin.

"Eva," Mrs. McConnell came out of the laundry room, wiping her hands on a towel. "I heard you were looking for me."

"Yes, I wanted to go over the order of events for the ceremony and celebration."

Unlike Mary and the duke, however, Mrs. McConnell did not smile. Instead, she regarded Eva warily for a long moment before jerking her chin toward the closet door. "Come with me. I need to gather a few things. We can talk while I work."

Eva's stomach threatened to sink, but she did as she was told. Neither of them spoke until they were in a little room filled with piles of linens and the door was not only shut, but wedged closed by Mrs. McConnell's broom. Then Mrs. McConnell turned to Eva and folded her arms across her chest.

"Alright, Miss Eva. I've only been around you for a couple of months, but I know you well enough to know that you wouldn't readily agree to this marriage even if it killed you. Now what are you up to?"

Eva hesitated. It was obvious that Mrs. McConnell wasn't going to believe her story, no matter what Eva said. And though Eva had always liked the kind housekeeper, as Mrs. McConnell had been one of the few servants willing to actually speak with her or have the audacity to empathize, she wasn't sure just how far the older woman's allegiances aligned with anyone.

"I need to know something."

"Yes?"

"Why do you work for the duke? Before you tell me that it's for the money, I know that's not true."

Mrs. McConnell tilted her head and studied Eva. "And what would make you say that?"

"I've seen the books. You make a large salary, but you spend very little of it." Eva took a deep breath. "And yet you wait on the duke hand and foot with more attention than I've ever seen a servant give their master. Before I tell you my secrets, I need at least one of yours."

Mrs. McConnell gave a small sigh and walked over to the window. She placed her hand against the pane and traced the frame with her finger.

"Carlton is my godson," she said in a quiet voice.

Eva stared at her. She had been entertaining a number of possibilities, but that hadn't been one of them.

"You needn't wonder at the oddity." Mrs. McConnell gave her a knowing smile. "The arrangement is indeed odd." She turned and grabbed a pile of linen and began folding it. "Before his parents were married, I was close friends with his mother. We worked in the same seamstress's shop, in fact. Then, one day when we were both nineteen, the duke's father, who was not yet the duke himself at that point, wandered in. The two fell in love at first sight, and it wasn't long before they were married and Carlton was on the way."

"So that's why the duke doesn't struggle with my lack of station," Eva said.

The housekeeper nodded. "His mother had no station either. But what she and his father did have was love. Unfortunately, by the time I needed work and was hired on here as the head house-keeper, she and her husband, while desperately attached to their little boy, had failed to give him any sort of proper discipline. The older he got, the more he created his own set of rules that he expected everyone around him to understand and follow."

Eva shifted uncomfortably. "This didn't bother his parents?"

"They thought he was brilliant. They encouraged it, even. Applauded it. His mother in particular. *Isn't he a brilliant boy?* they would say. *Doesn't he have the makings of a leader?*"

She shook her head and folded the linen shirt in her hands with a new ferocity. "The older he grew, the more obnoxious he became. Having several children of my own, I always found him a rather odd duck. I loved him, of course, as he was my godson, and I had watched him grow since infancy. But there was a pride about him that they failed to nip, and a strange sense of self-righteousness that I can only attribute to their heaping of constant praise. So believe me," she met Eva's gaze with a hard stare, "when I say that although I love the boy and always will, he is fit to be no one's master. And if I could undo all of the damage his parents accidentally inflicted upon this land when they died early and left him the title, I would do so in a heartbeat."

Eva frowned and grabbed a shirt to fold for want of something to do with her hands. "I'm curious then. Why did you stay?"

"I suppose I had always hoped to have the chance to undo what my friend began. But I never found that chance. Until now. So," she folded her hands and looked at Eva with the same expectant stare that her mother had often worn when she wanted one of the children to admit to something they had done, "is there something you would like to tell me? Or should I begin guessing and risk spoiling those well-made plans?"

Eva swallowed. Telling Mrs. McConnell of her plans was risky. Should the housekeeper be lying, the duke would find out and Eva would risk everyone and everything she had worked so hard to save. But . . . if there was a chance that the head housekeeper, the woman the duke trusted more than anyone else in the world, was telling the truth, Eva might just stand the chance of not only succeeding in her plans but executing them to the fullest. She stared hard at Mrs. McConnell for a long moment. She wasn't sure what she saw that convinced her exactly, but in the end, she knew she had to try.

"I would like to honor him with a song," she said slowly, "to express to him the depth of my most sincere emotions so that he might be privy to the honest love that fills my heart."

Mrs. McConnell began to smile. "And how might I help you in expressing such feelings?"

Eva couldn't stop the grin that spread across her face. She took the paper from her reticule that listed the order of events for the wedding ceremony and celebration. She held it up so that Mrs. McConnell could see the changes she had scratched on the paper.

"Right now, my betrothed has planned for me to demonstrate my abilities on the harp after the ceremony, during refreshments."

Mrs. McConnell looked at the paper. "So that's your only requested change?"

Eva grinned. "I would like to make sure that my song comes first."

I CAN EXPLAIN

*E*va drew in one shaky breath after another in an effort not to pass out. Part of her wondered why she hadn't done this before. The other part of her was screaming in her head, demanding to know why she was doing this at all. She didn't know how to control her magic. She didn't even like it! How, for all that was good and green, did she expect to beat the duke and his tangled plans?

She leaned a little farther out over the balcony's edge to try and see him better. He looked ridiculous in his green suit with all its puffs and frills and lace. Even the shoulders of his green suit were puffy. He swore it was all the rage in Astoria, but Eva highly doubted that.

At least he had let her wear white instead of green. He'd made a big fuss about it, of course.

"I'm not sure that would be appropriate after your little . . . tryst with Jack," he'd said the day before as a servant followed him around his study and tried to polish his fingernails whenever he quit moving, which wasn't often. "But I suppose I shall offer you the benefit of the doubt and let you continue with the white gown.

Wouldn't do for all the visiting dignitaries to think I was wedding a woman of loose morals."

Eva had colored at the insinuation, and had been very close to retorting that the duke's poetry had gone a good deal further in its musings than Jack had ever even approached in real life. But instead, she chose to change the subject.

No, nothing with Jack had ever truly transpired. And perhaps it was for the better. They would never see one another again. They couldn't. Not with Jack's life on the line. For if they ever did meet, even by accident, there was a good chance he would demand to know why she had turned him out. And she still wouldn't be able to tell him, tomorrow or twenty years later, as there had been no date of expiration on the contract, so she assumed it held power for the rest of her life.

Still . . . how she would have liked that kiss out on the balcony. They had been so close.

She was jarred from her thoughts as the duke ran over to one of the tables spread out across the lawn, dipped his finger right in a guest's goblet, and tasted it. The guest made a slight grimace but said nothing as the duke went on to describe in great detail all he knew about wine.

Pride, she nodded to herself, would be his downfall. He could plan all he wanted, but his excessive pride had made it rather easy for him to accept her act of defeat and believe her to be in love with him. After she had devised her plan and began acting as though she'd given up, the duke had really seemed to believe her. He'd even gone on to compose several new sonnets to read aloud to her as they prepared for the ceremony, each line worse than the last.

Well, he could have his awful sonnets. He could even think himself in love, and because of the contract, she would have to marry him in the end. But she would make sure that no one else would ever again have to suffer the consequences of her unwanted gift. Not now, not ever. They might die despising one another and as penniless as robins, should the duke be punished for his plotting, but she would not allow him to use her anymore.

Mrs. McConnell turned Eva toward the mirror as she had a few days prior during the fitting. Unlike last time, however, there was no sorrow in Mrs. McConnell's blue eyes. Only bright determination. She waved the other servant girls out of the room, then whispered in Eva's ear.

"Are you ready?"

Eva took a deep breath and then shook her head. "No. But let's go."

Mrs. McConnell escorted her to the side door, where they stood and waited for their signal to walk out onto the lawn. As they waited, Eva peeked through the window to get a glimpse of what was supposed to be her wedding. What she saw shocked her.

Hundreds of people sat out on the lawn in a semicircle, some on blankets and others on chairs from inside the mansion. They all faced the roofed platform that had been set up for the wedding where the officiant was preparing. Yellow climbing roses and vines with little white flowers covered the platform's sides so much that none of the actual wood was visible. Most of the people looked very thin, and some of the children were even chewing blades of grass. Eva's heart twisted as she watched them. This was her hour. Whether or not he had planned for a rebellion, he was going to get one. And it would be spectacular.

"Alright," Mrs. McConnell said. "It's time."

With a meaningful nod, Eva placed her arm on the older woman's once more. With her parents unavailable to present her to the groom, she had requested that Mrs. McConnell be her escort. The duke had been delighted.

"See?" He'd beamed at her. "You're finding your place here already. You'll be at home in no time!"

Eva smiled wryly to herself as she and Mrs. McConnell left the house and began the long walk toward the official presiding over the ceremony. Unlike some of the other kingdoms in the continent,

Eva had been notified that Guthwardians thought it was bad luck for the bride to walk directly toward the groom. Rather, the groom and the bride started off on opposite sides of the semicircle and walked around its perimeter, meeting together just before the officiant. Just running willy-nilly down the aisle was a disaster waiting to happen, one of the maids explained solemnly when Eva had asked. It demonstrated that the bride would do all the work. No, it was better if the groom had to work a little to get to the bride as well.

Well, that was fine with Eva. While she thought the superstition a bit absurd, it gave her a chance to see more of what she would be working with. She'd seen it the day before when she had walked around, innocently dropping seeds near the platform and around the house, but not since all the people had come. She hoped her seeds had been placed well, but it was too late to change anything either way.

For once, the fields surrounding them were empty. The workers had all been invited to the ceremony. Tables covered in food, which the vast majority of the guests were eyeing even now, filled the yard just behind the mansion. The day was hot and sticky, and the hum of cicadas filled the air. For miles, she could see nothing but the rolling red hills and the neat lines of green crops that covered them. Only a single road led to and from the mansion, and Eva was rather sure all the guests were accounted for. She just hoped those present would listen after she was finished. Who knew what the duke had told them?

As she neared the platform, she came to the guests seated at the front of the semicircle in chairs that had been brought out from the mansion. These were the nobles and aristocracy, she guessed. Not only were they seated in real chairs in front of the commoners present, but their appearances, largely fine jewels, ridiculously decorated hats, and tailored suits, were vastly different from those sitting on the ground behind them. Many of them were thin, but few looked as gaunt as the others. Eva could only guess that the rich had their food brought in daily from other regions, just as their guests had mentioned the week before.

A few of the faces were familiar. Eva recognized the moon-eyed woman, who was still staring at the duke as though she were the one getting married. Well, Eva thought, she could have him. Just not until after Eva was through teaching him a lesson.

Only one face stood out to her as particularly unusual as she neared the front of the crowd. The man was not very young, but not old either. He had dancing blue eyes, and though he wore finer clothes than any of the others, his skin was weathered by the sun. A small smile played on his lips, as though he found the whole thing amusing.

Could that be the king?

She didn't have time to dwell on her speculations, though, as she and the duke were fast approaching the officiant, despite her intentionally slow pace. A shiver ran down her back. She wasn't really sure she could do this. But she had no choice.

"Friends and guests," the duke turned to address the crowd, "I am grateful for your presence today to bear witness to my wedding."

Eva almost smiled.

"The order of events will be as follows," he continued. "After my bride and I share vows, we will sup. Then while everyone eats, you will bear witness to another great marvel. For I have found a way to defeat this wretched famine." He turned to Eva and took her hands in his clammy ones, giving her a smarmy smile. "And my bride holds the key."

The man Eva thought might be the king stopped smiling, and that's when Eva remembered the king's great dislike of anything magic. Well, if he hadn't been completely sure of his stance before, he would be after this.

"On that thought," Eva said, shyly turning to face the crowd as well, "I have a surprise for you, husband-to-be." She nearly choked on the words, but her act must have been at least half convincing, for after a moment of confusion, he broke into a radiant smile.

Eva beckoned at several servants standing in the shadow of a pecan tree, and they responded by carefully carrying out one of her harps and her little stool. After setting them gently beside her on the stage, they bowed and backed away. Eva waved her thanks and sat down. Placing her hands above the strings, she looked at the duke with the most adoring gaze she could force, and smiled.

"You've gifted me your songs and sonnets for weeks now in which you've poured out your heart. So I thought it was finally my turn to show you how I really feel." She let her smile harden just a hair. "What you deserve."

Eva closed her eyes and began to play. The song began innocently enough. A little bubbling melody, much like water gurgling in a stream or sparrows playing in a puddle. She could hear the audience gasp and then clap, and she knew that the flowers around her must have begun growing. She snuck a glance at the duke. His smile was confused, but he didn't seem suspicious. That meant it was time to turn the song.

She closed her eyes again and imagined a snake weaving its way through the leaves to the stream. Danger wove its way into the song, little tendrils of minor notes slipping in here and there. And as the song moved more and more toward the danger and away from the sweet chirps of birds and the happy chitter of squirrels, her fingers flew more violently across the strings. Faster and harder she played.

Someone cried out in the audience.

"What's happening?"

"What is she doing?"

"I thought magic was prohibited!"

"Eva!" the duke cried. His face was no longer serene or even confused. Instead, he looked panicked and angry. "What are you doing?"

Eva fixed him with a steady gaze as her fingers continued to play. "What I should have done long ago." Into her music she poured every ounce of sorrow she knew. But not only the sorrow. No, she went beyond the guidelines that Mortimer had set. Now she added anger. Betrayal. The need for justice.

Screams of terror erupted from all sides, but Eva continued to play.

"Eva! Stop!" the duke shouted.

Eva only played harder.

"Stop, or I'll kill Jack!"

The power that had been building inside her with each note she played crescendoed into a cacophony of sound, power, and light. For one long moment, she was one with her music and its power. She let the music carry her to a place in her heart she'd never been before. It was a place of strength and ownership and confidence. For the first time in her life, Eva had nothing to hide. Everything she was and knew and believed and had practiced for was shooting through the air for the world to see.

Then it was gone. No matter how hard she reached to find the magic, it was gone. She opened her eyes. People were either running down the road or hiding behind tables, chairs, or anything else that couldn't grow. The yellow roses were the size of dinner plates with thorns as long as Eva's forearms, and the little white flowers were as big as the roses had been to begin with. The grass was as tall as her knees. But most impressive, however, were the beanstalks.

Everywhere she'd dropped a seed the day before now had a beanstalk that reached up to the clouds. As thick as the duke's waist, they towered so high they blocked the sun from reaching much of the yard immediately surrounding the mansion. There were dozens spread out all over the place between the house, the pecan tree groves at the edge of the property, and the apple trees behind them. Still more were scattered randomly about the front and side yards.

"What's this about?" The man Eva had guessed to be the king

shoved the men around him, presumably his guards, aside and strode forward. He stopped at the foot of the stage and looked back and forth between them. "Carlton, why is your bride terrorizing your guests with magic?" He furrowed his dark brows at Eva. "Which is illegal, if she wasn't aware."

"I don't know, sire." The duke glowered at Eva.

"Because," the king continued, putting his hands behind his back, "as much as I should dislike arresting the bride, I will have to if I'm not provided an excellent explanation for all this." He gestured at the chaos around them.

Eva opened her mouth to plead her case, but then she stopped. She had hoped her plan would have somehow incapacitated the duke, though she really wasn't sure why she'd thought it would. Now she could say nothing. The duke could still kill Jack, and nothing would have been accomplished.

Some plan this had turned out to be.

"I can explain, sire."

Eva whirled around with the others to find Jack standing at the edge of the yard, holding a piece of parchment.

"Jack," she shook her head, "whatever you're doing, please go home. You'll only make things worse."

But Jack started toward them anyway. "I do know that the duke forced you to sign this contract." He held up the paper.

"Jack, please!"

"I also know," he continued, "that he threatened you with deadly consequences should you disobey him."

Eva's lungs squeezed as she tried to think of a way to stop him, if not for his own sake, then for the sake of the random stranger the contract had threatened as well.

"Jack, you need to stop!" Her voice was nearly hysterical.

"What in the blazes is this about?" The king turned to Jack. "Let me see that."

Jack handed the contract to the king, and Eva felt her heart shatter.

"Where did you get that?" the duke sputtered. "How?"

"Magic gives, but it also takes." Jack stared hard at the duke while the king read the contract. Finally, the king looked up, eyes blazing.

"Well, you've done a lot of rotten things in your life, cousin, but this is by far the worst." He flicked the paper. "Forced matrimony? Magic?" His eyes narrowed at the duke. "You're behind this famine as well, aren't you?" He turned to Eva. "My dear, is all of this true?"

Eva nodded as tears streamed down her face.

The king's face softened as he looked back and forth between Eva and Jack. "And this young man is—"

"Yes," Eva sobbed. She wrung her hands as she looked at Jack. He had struck her as handsome the first time they'd met, but now he was so much more. When she looked at him, she didn't see a square jaw and a fine straight nose. She saw empathy and kindness, a love for children, and strong hands to catch her and lift her back up whenever she might fall. In his slate-gray eyes, she saw a rock-solid determination to protect and keep. She saw a chest to cry into and a neck to snuggle against when the world was cold. A man she would be happy to spend forever with.

How had he found out today, of all days? Now, she had only until midnight. And then he would be gone as well.

"Arrest the duke," the king said. As his guards moved to obey, he grimaced at Carlton. "I have an idea that we'll be spending much time together, cousin, as long as it takes before you decide it behooves you to tell me what you were planning." He glanced at Eva again. "And why ever did you decide to kidnap her?" Then his voice hardened. "And how do we stop her poor fellow from dying? Really, Carlton, you were always odd, but this is just unthinkable!"

"I would have died," Jack spoke up, the ghost of a smile playing on his lips, "if my name was Jack."

THIS IS YOUR CHOICE

"*What?*" Everyone, including the duke, stared.

"My father's name," Jack spoke, his eyes never leaving Eva's, "was Jack. And as I grew older, I looked more and more like him, so everyone began calling me by his name, particularly my mother whenever she was angry with me. But my real name," his eyes began to twinkle, "is Phillip."

Eva stared at him. So many emotions crashed through her. Relief was the most overwhelming, and threatened to make her break down in tears again. Anger at his secrecy was simmering just beneath the relief, for all the unnecessary heartache she'd endured over the last few days. Joy that made her want to giggle foolishly.

Out of her eye, Eva noticed the duke reach into his coat. The king's men had already bound his wrists together, but they'd forgotten to bind his hands behind his back. Eva darted forward, knocking the duke to the ground. The little ball he'd shown her weeks before rolled from his hand. Eva scrambled to reach it, but the duke grabbed her ankle.

The king's men were on him in seconds, but from the duke's smile, Eva knew he had planned it this way.

"Jack!" she screamed, forgetting his real name as the ball rolled to Phillip's feet. "Don't touch it!"

"Let me go!" The duke's voice rose to a hysterical pitch. "Or I'll—"

Before the duke could finish whatever threat he was making, the sky shimmered, and a *bang* filled the air. To Eva's surprise, Mortimer appeared. He waved his hand at the duke, and a clump of dirt flew into the air and came down around the ball, burying it completely.

Eva looked at Mortimer in awe. He just grimaced back.

"Don't start thinking this is a common occurrence. I expect things to be the way between us that they were before, understand?"

Eva nodded and smiled. "I have just one request first."

He sighed dramatically. "And that would be?"

"I want this magic gone. Gone from me and my music. I want to be the way I was before."

He looked down at her as though she were dense. "But it is gone."

"What?"

Mortimer looked up at the beanstalks rising into the clouds. "You used it all on them."

"You mean . . ." She looked down at her hands and then the harp. "I'm not cursed anymore?"

He scowled. "You're no longer fairy-blessed, if that's what you mean. But don't ask for another gift ever again. I'm done with you, you hear?" He scratched his ear. "Your younger sister . . . the rotten one—"

"Sophie?"

"The wicked one, yes, has summoned me every day since you were gone and yelled about my 'irresponsibility' and all sorts of other mean things." He frowned at Eva. "I expect her to be the first one you notify when this whole thing is over. Understand?"

Eva grinned up at him. "Of course." She had thought he had a change of heart about his gift to her, but now she was wondering if all of his apparent repentance had merely been due to Sophie's harassment.

With that, Mortimer nodded once and then disappeared with a puff of smoke. Eva ran over to Jack and threw her arms around him, but before she could exclaim over her joy, the duke cleared his throat loudly. Everyone turned to look at him.

"This fellow here might have been saved by a technicality," he said, "but the life of the stranger is still in peril." He straightened as well as he could, despite the extra chains that had been put on his wrists. "You haven't wed the duke. And unless you do so now, someone will be dead by morning."

Eva felt nauseous. She had forgotten the other half of the contract. They had been so close to a perfect ending. And yet, she would still have to marry the duke.

"Keep it up, and *you'll* be dead by morning." Jack . . . or Phillip, rather, began to roll his sleeves up, but he was waved off by the king.

"As unfortunate as my cousin's scheming is," he said, cracking his knuckles, "I believe I have a way to fix this." He looked at Eva then Phillip. "The question is whether or not you two are willing to make the sacrifice in order to save the . . ." He looked back down at the parchment. "The life of whomever this unfortunate curse targets."

"What do you mean?" Phillip asked.

"By law, my cousin's actions have caused him to forfeit his title and property. And as he has no close family, I have the right to give said title and property to whomever I want."

Eva's heart gave an uneven beat. Was she hearing him correctly?

"I don't know either of you from the next person, but your actions today have proved the depth of your characters. Enough, at least, to satisfy me that your best interests are with that of the kingdom. So if you," the king turned to Phillip, "are willing to accept the title of duke and all the responsibilities that go with it, I'll name you duke here and now." He turned to Eva. "Unless, of course, there is another soul you would rather name duke and wed."

Eva's mouth suddenly felt dry. The king had just offered the duke's title to Jack . . . Phillip. And in doing such, he had offered them both not only a life together, but one of responsibility and wealth. They would never want for anything. Jack could escape his mother's clutches with his brothers, and Eva could be with the man she loved.

But that was all dependent on him. What if he didn't want to marry her? She'd been cruel when she'd sent him away. And now that his deal with Mortimer was off, he no longer had a responsibility to help her. Besides, he'd wanted to be a schoolmaster. He'd poked fun at most of the duke's noble friends whenever they'd come to visit, and now the king was asking him to not only be nobility, but also be first in line for the throne?

As she worried, staring at the ground, two rough hands took hold of hers and held them still. When she couldn't bring herself to look up, one of those hands moved to her chin and gently lifted her face. She found herself staring into his storm cloud–gray eyes.

And to her surprise, they looked terrified.

"I don't know what you had planned for your life after that winter ball," Phillip said softly, "but I know it wasn't this."

Eva let out what sounded like a strangled chuckle, odd even to her own ears.

"I know I'm just a farm boy, and you of all people know the kind of habits I need to break. But being with you this past month has made me want a life I never even knew existed." He paused to take a deep breath. Eva could barely bring herself to breathe as he took a small step closer. The heat from his hands traveled up her arms and across her face, making her blush as he continued to speak.

"This is your choice, though. I don't want anyone to ever force you into a certain life again, not the way he did." His voice softened as he ran his fingers along her jaw. "You've seen my good and my bad, much more than I wish you had. But if you'll have me, I'll be yours forever." Slowly, he dropped down on one knee.

"Eva . . . will you marry me?"

Before she knew what she was doing, Eva had thrown herself into Phillip's arms. And before she could say yes, he was kissing her. His lips melted against hers, and the way he enfolded her in his thick arms, nearly crushing her to his chest, was intoxicating. As one of his hands moved down to the small of her back and the other one cradled her face, she was vaguely aware of the king's laughter, but her thoughts were too abuzz to care.

Phillip was hers.

She had taken a chance.

She had lived.

The duke had been defeated.

And she would never hide again.

EPILOGUE

WE CHOOSE LOVE

*D*ear Rynn,

I'm sorry I wasn't able to send this sooner, but tracking you down has been more difficult than I thought. Hopefully this arrives before the cold weather, but if not, I suppose you can always guess what's gone on after.

Oh, how I've missed you. In all the time we spent talking at night, imagining what our lives would look like one day, I never pictured a future without you there by my side, telling me what you thought of my groom long before he was that. I especially didn't imagine a future where you were absent from my wedding. But so goes life, I suppose.

You would have hated my wedding gown. It was poofy everywhere but the sleeves, and I probably looked like an over-frosted pastry. I have to say, however, that I'm more fond of it than I thought I would be. And ~~Jack~~ Phillip was as handsome as ever in his farmer's clothes.

You would like that about him. Actually, I think you would like a lot about him, possibly because in many ways, he reminds me of you. He dislikes pretenses, and just as you predicted about my future husband, he doesn't care a lick about my height. In truth, he's only an inch or so taller than me. But really, it's quite nice, as I always thought my height might end my chance at romance before it ever began.

I'm not sure where you'll be when you get this letter, but if you hear of the Duke and Duchess of Guthward and any awkward situations they might cause, be kind. Mother trained me for many things, but to be a duchess was never one of them. After we were married, the king even let on with a gleam in his eye that we should take care of any children we have.

"You never know if they might end up as kings or queens one day," he said with a grin. I'm still under the impression that he will one day find a woman to tame his wild ways, but ~~Jack~~ Phillip isn't so sure. He says the king is as in love with adventure, according to the local gossip, as any man ever was with a woman. Sure, he's dabbled in love and even proposed several times, but no woman would ever put up with his eternal wandering. Time will tell, I suppose.

In the meantime, we're back in Astoria. Father found us an adorable little cottage just outside the market. The king agreed to allow a kindly baron and his wife to live in the duke's mansion and carry out his responsibilities while ~~Jack~~ Phillip attends the university here. He has always wished to continue his learning, and while the king insisted that he take classes in economics, politics, and agriculture, the duke's estate will also allow us to afford classes in education for children, which is what ~~Jack~~ Phillip has always dreamed of doing.

I will admit some concern about his mother. I had the unpleasant pleasure of meeting her soon after we arrived in Astoria (another story for another day), and I hope I never have to again. She's even worse than he made her sound. Thankfully, his brothers have been moved to the duke's mansion, where the head housekeeper has taken to spoiling them rotten. And while his mother was greatly displeased with this, the king allowed them to be removed for ~~Jack's~~ Phillip's concern that they'll not be fed and looked after properly without him. He offered to send money to pay for workers until she's able to get the farm producing again, but she's not content to let her son grow rich without her. I get the feeling I shall have to learn to be rather fierce with her. The good news is that she acts enough like a small child that I can pretend she is one and then treat her as such without remorse. While I'm still learning to create boundaries with adults, naughty children I have no qualms with rebuking. And she is indeed much like a naughty, pouty, spoiled little girl.

Is it terribly awful of me to find it quite funny that Mortimer forgot to remove the rabid cat he placed on their farm to protect them? No, don't answer that.

His mother aside, I shall be taking up my harp again. I was kindly given another invitation to play at the Winter Ball this year, and as I apparently broke Mortimer's spell, I have enjoyed playing more than ever. (Although, there are days when I could swear the plants outside my window are a few inches taller after I've played. The servants say I'm not the only one who notices it, either.) I'm also teaching myself flute, lyre, and the violin, and while ~~Jack~~ Phillip (I'm not sure I'll ever get used to that) is in school, I shall be teaching music to several children in the neighborhood as well. We don't need the money now, I suppose, but I detest the idea of sitting still like a glass doll on display all day.

King Eston, as much as he despises magic in general, hired several well-known professors of magic from the university to help him understand the duke's plans. While I was under his thumb, the duke forced me to play music on two different harps twice a day, music to grow plants in the morning and music to kill them at night. Apparently, he had positioned the harps that he forced me to use so that the one I played in the morning would grow his crops. The one I played at night was positioned so it echoed off the mountain and overshot his fields, hitting the vast majority of the rest of Guthward. That my magic was not only able to exist with the thick red clay of Guthward's soil but also affect the whole kingdom is a testament to just how strong Mortimer's magic was that he gifted me with. I can only assume it was another one of his experiments.

The professors also said that the magic baubles the duke liked to keep around the house, and the contract he created to threaten ~~Jack~~ Phillip with, were purchased in other kingdoms and would have been much stronger had he not been in Guthward. One of the professors of magic said since I used pure emotion to break the spell, I must have been feeling rather strongly about the duke and his plans.

Apparently, he's never heard one of the duke's love songs.

Anyhow, in using me to starve the rest of the kingdom and speed the growth of his own crops, the duke planned to move in and prove his qualification to be king by ending the famine using magic. My magic. He was very close to succeeding, too, as many of the nobles had been ready to vote for him rather than give confidence to the king. His games seem to have bitten him in the behind, however, as he is now in prison and no longer a duke, and the king's authority is more respected than ever. Also, much of the kingdom is as suspicious of magic now as the king ever was.

From what we can gather, after finding out about Mortimer's gift, the duke searched for any family we might have in Guthward. Sure enough, he found Tamra. Tamra had no qualms about selling me out. Even after I was kidnapped, she was charged by the duke with keeping Mother, Father, and everyone else looking in the wrong places and feeding them bad information. And while I know the two of you were never close, don't try sending her correspondence any time soon. She's in prison, now, as well. ~~Jack~~Phillip and I will be caring for her children for the time being, which we are quite delighted about.

You'll be proud to know that I've finally discovered what it means to live. As soon as I'd been reunited with our family, I promptly ordered another version of the dress I gave away. But this time, it's red. Unfortunately, or fortunately, however you decide to look at it, I won't be wearing the dress any time soon, though.

Being with child makes everyday clothes rather tight, or so I've been told. I suppose I shall find out, as Phillip (I finally got it!) and I will be welcoming our first baby into the world sometime next summer. Hopefully, you won't be too far away by then, as I want this baby and his or her auntie to be very well acquainted.

To be honest, living as a duchess and very possibly a queen was never the way I envisioned the future. But I've found that I'm more than at peace with this new life. I'm loving it. From the time I wake up in the morning to when I lay down my head, it seems life never slows but instead continues to speed by. And yet I'm finding great joy even in the little everyday details. And while we can't say what will happen in the future, we're hoping to open the ducal mansion one day as a house for orphans. ~~Jack~~ (Oh fiddlesticks, I did it again) Phillip can teach them reading and sums when he's not managing the estate, and I can teach them music and tuck them all into bed at night.

You worried once that I would never find a man worthy of me (which was a silly worry if I ever heard one). You would love my husband. He's everything I ever dreamed of and more. He's stubborn and kind and always keeping an eye out for those around him. Again, he reminds me so much of you, it's probably why I love him so. Ever since I told him about the baby, he's been worried sick about me. I'm not allowed to so much as move a footstool across the room, even though I'm not even showing yet.

Of course, he has some rather irksome habits, such as chewing with his mouth open and falling onto the bed without removing his boots. But we all have our faults, I suppose, and he is a good man. Such a good man.

My other main concern is Sophie. Since we've finally gotten locations sorted out, I've been talking with Mother and Father again, and it appears that Father has it in his mind that Sophie would be better off married young to a farmer or in his words, "a fellow of stable employment." I can only hope Sophie doesn't do something rash.

Oh dear. The more I think about it, the more I'm convinced that Sophie's going to do something rash.

Well, before I worry myself to death, I'll end by putting your former worries to rest at least. Phillip and I haven't known one another for very long, but we made an agreement the first night of our marriage that we were going to choose love. Through hard times and high times, we will choose mercy and hope and love. But most importantly we choose love. Because when the world seems to take away every other choice in our life and tries to convince us that all is lost, we can always choose love.

I miss you more than you can know. Come home as soon as you can, and take care with your travels. Until then, however, you always have my heart.

Love,
    Eva

~

And To Kitty, Shari, Kenley, Aya, and Melanie…

You ladies are the best cheer squad a girl could ask for. Except, we don't know any cheers, and instead of pom poms, we post .gifs with reckless abandon. So here's to sneaking sword fights into contemporary romances, and vanquishing our enemies with pictures of naked cats. Eventually, we'll get our girls' day out!

ENTWINED TALES CONTINUES WITH
SOPHIE'S STORY

A Bear's Bride: A Retelling of East of the Sun, West of the Moon by Shari L. Tapscott.

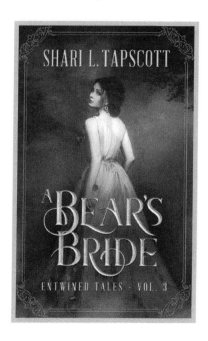

Don't judge a prince by his fur.

After her father threatens to marry her to a dull farmer, free-spirited Sophie runs away from the only home she's ever known and sets off into the world, seeking adventure and romance. But instead of excitement, she finds a forlorn castle and the solitary prince who lives there.

For twenty years, Henri has been shrouded in mystery and speculation. He's a legend, a nightmare, a blight upon his fair kingdom. Though Sophie knows it would be wiser to return home, she's inexplicably drawn to the man of shadows.

But it doesn't take Sophie long to realize that falling for the cursed prince might prove to be more of an adventure than she ever bargained for...

Entwined Tales

ENTWINEDTALES.COM

Everyone wishes they had a fairy godmother to make the world a little more magical... They've never met Mortimer.

Every good deed merits a reward, at least according to the Fairy Council. But when a kind woodcutter's family is rewarded with a grumpy, sarcastic, irresponsible fairy godfather named Mortimer, their lives are changed forever... and not in a good way.

Follow the woodcutter's seven children as Corynn, Eva, Sophie, Elisette, Martin, Anneliese, and Penelope head out into the world to find adventure, new friends, and their very own happily-ever-afters. Their greatest challenge? Avoiding their fairy godfather's disastrous attempts to help.

Welcome to the Entwined Tales—six interconnected fairy tale retellings by authors KM Shea, Brittany Fichter, Shari L. Tapscott, Kenley Davidson, Aya Ling, and

Melanie Cellier. Join the fun and enter the brand new world of the Entwined Tales for six enchanting stories filled with humor, magic, and romance.

AFTERWORD

Thank you for reading An Unnatural Beanstalk. I hope you enjoyed it!

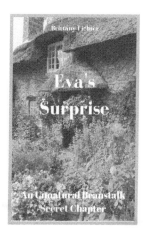

If you like exclusive content (including a secret chapter about Phillip and Eva), you can visit <u>BrittanyFichterFiction.com</u> and join my no-spam newsletter for free access to secret chapters, sneak peeks at books before they're published, release announcements, and much more!

Also, if you enjoyed An Unnatural Beanstalk, it would be a HUGE help to me if you left an honest review on Amazon or at Goodreads.com. Reviews help authors sell more books, allowing them, in turn, to write more! Thank you!

Also by Brittany Fichter...

The Classical Kingdoms Collection
Before Beauty: A Retelling of Beauty and the Beast
Blinding Beauty: A Retelling of The Princess and the Glass Hill
Beauty Beheld: A Retelling of Hansel and Gretel
Girl in the Red Hood: A Retelling of Little Red Riding Hood
Silent Mermaid: A Retelling of The Little Mermaid
Cinders, Stars, and Glass Slippers: A Retelling of Cinderella

～

The Classical Kingdoms Collection Novellas
The Green-Eyed Prince: A Retelling of the Frog Prince

～

The Autumn Fair Trilogy
The Autumn Fairy
The Autumn Fairy of Ages
The Last Autumn Fairy

ABOUT THE AUTHOR

Brittany lives with her Prince Charming, their little fairy, and their little prince in a ~~sparkling~~ (decently clean) castle in whatever kingdom the Air Force has most recently placed them. When she's not writing, Brittany can be found enjoying her family (including their spoiled black Labrador), doing chores (she would rather be writing), going to church, belting Disney songs, exercising, or decorating cakes.

Facebook: Facebook.com/BFichterFiction
Subscribe: BrittanyFichterFiction.com
Email: BrittanyFichterFiction@gmail.com
Instagram: @BrittanyFichterFiction
Twitter: @BFichterFiction

Made in the USA
Coppell, TX
30 June 2020

29640323R00118